RULE #4: YOU CAN'T TRUST THE BAD BOY

THE RULES OF LOVE SERIES

ANNE-MARIE MEYER

Sweet Heart Books

To my Dad

Join my Newsletter!

Find great deals on my books and other sweet romance!

Get, Fighting Love for the Cowboy FREE

just for signing up!

Grab it HERE!

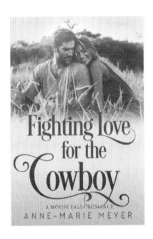

SHE'S AN IRS AUDITOR DESPERATE TO PROVE HERSELF.

HE'S A COWBOY TRYING TO HOLD ONTO HIS RANCH.

LOVE WAS NOT ON THE AGENDA.

CHAPTER ONE

I'll never get used to the out-of-body feeling you experience when the plane descends out of the sky. The feeling of your stomach staying put as you drop to earth always made me feel like I was going to throw up. Or maybe it was because I was returning home.

I was never really sure.

Pressing my hand to my stomach, I forced myself to close my eyes and picture what was waiting for me when the plane landed.

What a joke.

Mom and Dad weren't going to be there. They couldn't be bothered to pick me up. They'd probably send Theodore or Jackson, or some other random person that they just hired to take care of the daughter they forgot about.

I was their only child, and yet I was the one person they couldn't seem to remember existed.

Until they wanted something.

"Thanks for riding with us, Ms. Brielle," Maria, my family's flight attendant, said as she nodded at me from her seat.

I smiled at her. "It was a great ride." Emphasis on the sarcasm.

I'm terrified of heights, but my parents don't care. It's mandatory. The ceremonial flight into Atlantic City from New York every year for the summer. When I tried to tell Mom that I hated flying, she scoffed and told me to take a Valium.

Thanks, Mom.

But sadly, she was serious. She actually sent a doctor to my dormitory to remind me how in control of my life she is, even when she's not around. Even one hundred plus miles away, she dictates what type of medicine I take or the way I spend my time.

The plane touched down with a thunk, and I watched the scenery pass by as we taxied into the hanger. Once we stopped moving and the stairs were brought, I unbuckled and got out of my seat. Maria tried to beat me to my suitcase, but I got there first.

I curled my fingers around the handle and shot her another smile despite her disgruntled expression.

"Thanks, Maria. I'll see you once summer is over?"

Maria nodded as she pinched her lips into a tight line and straightened her skirt. "Of course, Ms. Brielle. That's what we're here for."

Captain Bob popped his head out of the cockpit to bid me farewell as I headed down the stairs. I waved my hand in his direction and descended to the hangar floor just in time to see a man in a dark suit walk over to me.

"Good morning, Ms. Brielle. I'll be taking you to the hotel today."

I nodded, and, before I could protest, he grabbed my luggage and started wheeling it over to the BMW parked off to the side. I sighed as I followed after him.

Here we go.

My summer was most certainly packed with the responsibilities and galas that are required to be a Livingstone. We were in the hotel business, so image was everything. And my parents spared no expense.

The ride to the Livingstone Hotel in central Atlantic City flew by. I kept my gaze out the window and my hands clenched in my lap. I was dreading the next few months. I missed school. I missed my friends. I missed being noticed.

At home, my parents were all about work. They barely noticed me even when I was standing in their way.

I was invisible to them.

My phone chimed. I glanced down to see it was Kate, my best friend and the only person I hung out with while I was here. I smiled as I reached down and pressed the talk button.

"Hey."

A loud squeal made me jerk the phone away from my ear. I could always count on her to be excited that I was home.

"You're here!" she cheered.

I laughed. "I'm here."

"Okay, call me once you've seen your parents, and we can hang out."

I nodded as I closed my eyes. I missed her, and I was grateful that she was there to help me navigate my relationship with the people who gave me life.

"Will do."

"We're going to par-tay," she sang out. "I gotta run. I'm needed at the ice cream shop. Call me later?"

"Yep," I said as a smile spread across my lips.

She sang her goodbye, and I pulled my phone from my cheek and hit the end call button. The screen went dark, and I slipped my phone into my purse. The car felt too quiet. I hugged my chest as I watched my chauffeur pull into the entrance of the hotel and stop at the large, glass doors.

He turned and smiled at me. "Welcome home."

I nodded as I pushed open the door and stepped out. Like magic, a valet appeared, pulled my suitcase from the trunk, and walked over to me.

"Ms. Livingstone, you're here," he said, giving me a huge smile.

My cheeks were hurting now. I'd definitely smiled more today than I had in the entire school year. There was something about being the boss's daughter that made everyone super happy around you. Or at least, gave them a reason to fake being happy.

Everyone was always fake around me. I could never tell if people were just being nice so they didn't get fired.

"Thanks," I said as I followed after him into the hotel lobby.

A cliché elevator song filled the silence as we rose thirty stories to the penthouse. My home.

Ha. Home had such hollow meaning to me.

Thankfully, the valet seemed to sense that I wasn't feeling chatty, so he didn't try to fill the tense ride with meaningless chatter.

I mean, did he really want to hear how my school year was? Or how my plane ride was?

No. He didn't care about that at all.

The elevator doors opened into a small hallway. At the end of it was a keypad door. I leaned down and grabbed my suitcase, pulling it away from the valet.

"I can take it from here," I said as I made my way through the open doors.

"But, your mother—"

"She'll be fine," I called over my shoulder. "I'm a big girl. I can carry in my own suitcases."

The elevator doors closed on his disgruntled expression, but he didn't march out and demand that he take over. Probably because Mom and Dad weren't around. Had they been standing there, it would have been a different story.

Now alone, I took a deep breath.

This was the summer before my senior year of high school. I was going to make the most of it. I wasn't going to let Mom and Dad push me around like they always did.

I was going to enjoy my break. Hang out with Kate and actually see some of Atlantic City the way a person should. Despite the fact that Mom would stare at me and tell me I'm crazy to want to socialize with locals. 'Cause who would want to do that?

I was tired of living this rich life they'd made for me. I wanted a real life.

I was ready to fall in love, despite my total lack of possibilities. I was a believer. If I wished hard enough, it just might happen.

After I punched in the code, the door unlocked and I headed inside.

Of course, the suite was pristine. Large windows lined the living room, allowing light to spill in and glisten off the marble countertops and the chandeliers hanging from the ceiling.

White furniture was adorned with red and yellow pillows—to add a splash of color in the room. And a dark fur rug rested on top of dark wood floors.

I rolled my suitcase inside and allowed the door to shut behind me.

"I'm home," I called out to no one in particular. Knowing Mom and Dad, they weren't here and wouldn't be for a while.

The clicking of heels sounded from the far rooms, and I knew right away who it was. Mrs. Porter. My mom's assistant. I'd recognize the sound of her shoes anywhere.

"Brielle," she exclaimed when she came into view.

I walked over and embraced her. She was more of a mother to me than my own mom.

"Jackie," I said, throwing my arms around her.

She pulled back and ran her gaze over me. Her familiar

black glasses sat perched on her nose. Her dark hair was greying and, as always, pulled back into a bun at the nape of her neck. "You look so grown up," she said.

I smiled at her. She hadn't changed. Every year, she told me how grown up I looked. "I'm eighteen in just a few weeks," I said as I tucked my strawberry blonde hair behind my ear.

She nodded, waving her hand at me to get me to stop talking. "Don't remind me," she said. "Because if you're that old, that means I'm..." She shook her head as she walked over to the fridge and pulled out two water bottles. "That means I'm twenty-five."

I took the bottle she handed me and nodded. "Right. And you've been twenty-five for how long now?"

She shushed me as I twisted the cap off and took a sip. Once I was done, I glanced around.

"I'm guessing they're out?" I waved my hand around the house.

Mrs. Porter's face fell as she nodded. "Meetings. I'm supposed to tell you to settle in and then make yourself presentable. Apparently there is a big lunch meeting they want you to attend."

I pressed my hand to my chest in a mocking way. "Me?"

She swatted my arm. "Yes, you."

I shrugged. Mrs. Porter hated when I talked about my parents negatively. But she only worked for them. I had to live with them. They were my only family and the only family I was ever going to have.

I sighed, not wanting to get into a battle with her again,

and walked over to my suitcase. "I'll go get ready," I said as I made my way over to my room.

"I've got to go too. Your mom will be out of her meeting shortly." She adjusted her glasses. "You'll be okay?"

I nodded and waved her away. "I'll be fine. I'm used to being on my own." I saluted her and then disappeared down the hall.

I snorted as I walked into my room. There was literally nothing here that resembled me. My daybed was still perfectly made—with a comforter I didn't recognize and would have never picked out.

My posters were gone, which I wasn't too heartbroken about. Even my bulletin board that had been full of pictures of me and Kate from last summer had vanished. It was like my parents wanted to remove any semblance of me from this room.

But I wasn't surprised. Mom did this every year. I assume she viewed it as being thoughtful, but it just felt morbid. Like I'd died or something.

She called it a fresh start—I called it getting rid of Brielle.

I left my suitcase at the entrance to my room and then made my way over to the bed and flopped down. I buried my face into the bright pink comforter and sighed.

Welcome home.

I flipped to my back and stared up at the ceiling. I tapped my fingers on my stomach as I brought my leg up and hummed some notes into the silent room.

This summer was going to be different. I was going to be

Brielle Livingstone, teenage girl. Not Brielle Livingstone, heiress to the Livingstone empire. I was going to figure out a way to become someone different.

I was going to *live*.

———

Despite all of my mental affirmations from earlier, I knew I had to attend this mysterious lunch I'd been summoned to, so I showered and toweled off my hair.

After a quick glance into my closet, I settled on a floral summer dress that highlighted my legs—my best asset, which was thanks to Mom. I dressed and got started with my makeup. Just as I finished applying my mascara, Mom walked in.

She was staring at her phone as she made her way into the center of my room and stopped.

I turned and gave her a smile. "Hey, Mom."

Growing up, I was always told that I looked like a minia-ture version of her. We both had strawberry blonde hair, bright blue eyes, and long legs. It felt weird to be told I had my mother's legs, but I eventually got over it.

Cause Mom had great legs.

Her hair was pulled back into a stylish braid, and she wore a deep-blue pencil skirt and a crisp white blouse. Her black heels sunk into my high-pile rug.

"Brielle, welcome home."

The standard Livingstone greeting.

"Thanks. Where's Dad?"

She glanced up at me, and then her gaze lowered to study my clothes. The look on her face told me she was not happy about my choice of wardrobe. "He's meeting us in the restaurant—is that what you are wearing?"

I glanced down at my dress. "Yes. Why?"

She scrunched up her nose. "You don't have anything nicer?"

"Nicer? Why? What is this meeting about?" It was strange they even wanted me there. Normally, I was only invited to functions so we could look like a quintessential American family. Just more proof that, to my parents, I'm a prop.

Mom sighed as she glanced down at her phone and then back up to me. "We're going to be late...just wear it. Come on. Let's go."

I finished brushing my fingers through my hair and stood. I quickly slipped into a pair of flats, despite my mom's very obvious sigh. There was no way I was going to this mystery meeting in uncomfortable heels I could barely walk in.

I followed Mom out of the room and over to the front door.

We headed out of the suite and stood by each other as we waited for the elevator to come. I fiddled with my dress, wishing Mom had let me bring my purse. But she always told me that it made me look desperate and poor, so I hadn't bothered to try to convince her otherwise.

Instead, I'd shoved my phone and debit card into my bra earlier, and, right now, my phone was digging into me.

"Stop fidgeting," Mom said as the elevator doors slid open.

I nodded and pressed my hands into my side as I followed after her. We turned to face the doors as they shut, and the elevator descended. The silence felt deafening, and I couldn't help but glance over at her.

At least the people they paid to wait on me asked me how my day was. It never seemed like Mom could be bothered. Which was fine. It's not like I wasn't used to it by now.

The elevator doors opened, revealing the lobby. People were bustling around, either in flip-flops and shorts, or pressed suits and briefcases. There was such a difference between people here for work and people here for vacation.

I wondered what I looked like to the people who glanced over at me as I walked by. Did I look like a tourist? A resident? I doubted I looked like I belonged. I never felt like I did.

But I didn't have time to let my thoughts wander too much. Mom turned and pressed her hand on my shoulder just before we walked into the restaurant. "Please understand that we are doing this for your future."

I stared at her. That was weird. "It's just lunch, Mom."

She glanced at me and nodded. "Right." Then she sucked in her breath. "But keep an open mind, okay?"

Worry sank in my stomach as I noticed the turmoil in her gaze. I knew my parents were strange, I just hadn't realized they were that strange.

"Okay, I promise."

Her gaze drifted down to her hand on my shoulder for a

moment before she tapped it a few times—a typical Lily Livingstone hug—and then smiled at me.

"All right. Let's get this done."

I don't know what I expected to see when Mom led me past the hostess stand and into the restaurant. Maybe the grim reaper. Maybe my grandmother sitting at our table, dressed in black and holding a rosary while she muttered prayers under her breath.

From the way Mom was going on, you'd think they were ordering me to my death or something.

But nothing seemed out of place. The restaurant was as bright and cheery as it had always been. The sun beat in through the floor-to-ceiling windows, causing tiny bursts of starlight on the walls from the crystal that was perfectly arranged on every white-clothed table.

I glanced over at Mom, wondering why she'd been so cryptic. I would have figured that an evil monster had taken over The Livingstone and turned it into the scourge of Atlantic City.

But nothing seemed amiss. In fact, the restaurant was unusually crowded for a Saturday afternoon in May.

"Why am I here?" I asked, leaning over and dropping my voice.

Mom shook her head as she pressed her finger to her lips and led me through the tables. "Hush, Brielle."

I stared at her. Since when did she shush me? My parents never really disciplined me. They were always too busy.

"They're here," she whispered as she turned to stare me down.

Call me crazy, but I didn't like the way she said, *they're here.* Suddenly, the only thing I wanted to do was run out of the room. Mom was up to something, and I wasn't going to like it.

CHAPTER TWO

I glanced behind my mom and saw two guys sitting at my parents' VIP table. There was an older man with greying hair and another man with darker hair, but that was all I could see since his back was to me.

"Who's here?" I asked with what I hoped came across as nonchalance.

Mom gave me a look as she adjusted her dress, pinched her cheeks, and then turned her obsessive personality onto me.

"I really wish you'd worn your hair up," she said as she started primping my curls and pinching *my* cheeks.

"Mom, please," I said, holding up my hands so she would stop. It was humiliating that she was acting this way. I wasn't a little kid anymore. In a few weeks, I would be eighteen. But right then, you would have thought I was a little kid with popsicle-dyed lips and ratty hair.

"I'm sorry. I just want you to look nice," she said as she took a deep breath.

I narrowed my eyes at her. "Why?"

She pinched her lips together. I couldn't tell if she was trying to work her lipstick into submission or trying to keep a secret. A nauseating feeling settled in my stomach—I feared it was the latter.

"Why am I here? What did you do?" I asked as Mom plastered on her fake smile and started to turn.

If she heard me, she didn't show it. Instead, she walked away from me and toward whatever impending doom loomed in front of me.

Great.

I glanced toward the exit and, for a moment, wondered if I could make it there before anyone saw me.

"Brielle, join us, please," Mom said in her *company's here* voice.

Too late. I resigned myself to the fact that retreat was not an option. I glanced longingly at the door one more time before I clenched my jaw and forced myself to head toward the VIP table. I just needed to get through whatever this lunch was and then get the heck out of there. I'd survive this. After all, I'd been pretty much on my own since I was a kid.

"Hello," I said in a sugary-sweet voice. I stepped up next to Mom and turned my smile toward the two men sitting at the table.

It was like staring at twins—if they had been born a few decades apart. The younger one looked about my age. He had dark hair and olive skin. His dark eyes lit up as his gaze roamed over me. A few seconds later, he was out of his seat and reaching over the table to take my hand.

"Hello," he said. His voice hinted to an Italian accent. "My name is Stefano Esposito."

I stared at his hand, which extended from a perfectly tailored suit. He looked as if he'd stepped out of an Italian GQ. My gaze flicked over to Mom, who was smiling so hard, it looked as if the edges of her lips were about to disappear into her hair.

"Be polite," she said quietly as she nudged me with her shoulder.

I glanced back at Stefano and nodded as I shook his hand. "Brielle," I said.

Stefano's smile widened to reveal perfectly white teeth. I couldn't help but stare at how bright they were, sparkling back at me.

"It's incredible to meet you," he said as he squeezed my hand.

I nodded as I wiggled my fingers loose from his grip. He settled back into his chair as I pulled out mine. Before I could reach down and pull my chair forward, a waiter appeared to help me.

Once I was situated, Dad showed up. His face was red, and beads of sweat formed on his brow as he nodded to Mom and me and then turned to the Espositos.

"Sorry for keeping you," he said as he waved down the waiter and ordered a scotch. "I had a disturbance to take care of," he muttered under his breath.

I peeked over to see Mom's face redden as she pulled her lips into a perfectly manicured line. No doubt she was not happy that Dad was drinking in the middle of the day, but there was no way she was going to say anything about that. Not in front of guests.

Wondering if I should push her, I contemplated ordering a grande sundae when the waiter asked for our orders, but I decided against it. It wasn't like I would even have a say in any of this. Mom ordered for me before I could get two words out.

I felt like pulling out my driver's license to remind Mom that I was no longer a baby. But knowing her, she'd just sigh and tell me that I was being difficult. Again.

Feeling stifled, I glanced around, wondering why I ever came back. At least in New York, I had a school I loved and friends who cared about me. Mom tried to control me there, but I could always hang up the phone. When I was here, my parents weren't even around long enough to ask me how my day was or what my plan for college was. Nothing.

"Talk to Stefano," Mom hissed as she leaned toward me.

That snapped me from my thoughts. I glanced over to her to see her nod in Stefano's direction. I didn't like that she was plotting something without cluing me in. I took a deep breath as I stared back at her.

"Now," she mouthed, accentuating the "o" with her bright red lips.

Defeated, I turned to find Stefano grinning at me. I

reached out and fiddled with the silverware on the table. After pulling out the cloth napkin, I slipped it onto my lap.

"So, have you been in the US long?" I asked as I smiled over at him.

Stefano nodded. "I've been studying business at Harvard for the last year. My father wants me to learn from the best schools."

I feigned interest. "Wow. Harvard. Nice."

Well, this was highly suspect. It was obvious that the Espositos were rich, and that meant this was a job. My parents wanted something from them. The fact that they insisted I be here...I stifled a groan. This was not good.

"I need to go to the bathroom," I said as I set my napkin onto my plate and stood.

Mom's hand engulfed mine. "Are you sure it can't wait?"

I stared down at her. Was she serious? "No. It can't," I said, leaning toward her, hoping she'd pick up on my tone.

Mom looked as if she were wrestling an alligator as she glanced at the Espositos and then back at me. She sighed and nodded toward the bathroom. "Go and come back."

I slipped my hand from hers and nodded. "I will," I said with a poor attempt to hold back my frustration.

Thankfully, Mom didn't notice the snap to my tone as she returned to talking to Stefano, Senior. I took her moment of distraction as my chance to get the heck out of here. I weaved through the tables in the direction of the bathroom—but I slipped into the lobby instead.

The Livingstone Casino and Hotel was huge. It had been passed down from generation to generation. It was the crown jewel of the Livingstone empire, and the lobby was just as formidable as the pride my family held for it.

Large floor-to-ceiling windows filled the front of the hotel, allowing a perfect view of the ocean. A large chandelier floated above me, catching every ray of sunshine and projecting them all over the place.

I leaned against the nearest wall and took a few deep breaths. I wasn't sure what my parents were plotting, but whatever it was, I didn't like it. When it came to business, my parents were ruthless.

Two security guards drew my attention as they made their way out of the casino on the other side of the foyer. It made me wonder if this was the disturbance Dad had been talking about earlier.

Right behind the two guards, two men appeared. The younger one—the one in a leather jacket and with dark, almost black, hair—had his arm wrapped around the shoulders of the older-looking man with matching hair.

The older man was pitched forward. His skin was pale, and he looked as if he hadn't seen the sun for a very long time. The younger one look disgruntled as he helped who I could only assume was his dad out into the lobby.

"We told you to keep him out of here," Horace, one of the security guards, said.

The boy flicked his gaze up to Horace and nodded. "It won't happen again," he said.

As he drew closer, I couldn't help but stare at him. He had dark green eyes and his hair kept falling over his forehead. I was pretty sure I'd seen him around a few times, but it wasn't like Dad let me associate with the locals.

Just as he passed by, he glanced over at me. His lips were drawn into a tight line. One that rivaled my mother's. Embarrassed, I turned my gaze to the floor to study the Italian marble that lay at my feet.

What was I doing? Why was I staring at this stranger?

Nervous, I slowly peeked back up only to find that he'd made his way through the doors and out onto the sidewalk. Horace and his buddy must have been satisfied that they'd gotten rid of him because they didn't follow him out.

Horace stood a few feet away from me with his arms folded.

"Psst." I leaned forward, hoping I could get Horace's attention. When he didn't respond, I tried again. "Horace," I whispered louder.

Horace turned and studied me. "What do you want, Ms. Livingstone?"

Ugh. When he said my name like that, it made me feel like my mother. I shivered at the thought and then decided to push it far from my mind. "Who is that?" I asked, nodding in the direction of the two guys who'd been escorted out.

Horace followed my gesture and then glanced back at me. "Why do you want to know?"

I tried not to groan and instead shrugged like I didn't care. "No reason. I've just never seen them around here before."

Horace turned so he was facing me. His normally tight

shoulders had relaxed, which seemed strange. He was a naturally uptight kind of guy.

"The drunk goes by Miller. He slums it up around town. Mostly getting in way over his head at the tables." Horace nodded toward the casino.

I waited, hoping he'd bring up the younger guy, who was, let's be real, the only one I was interested in.

"The kid holding him up is his son. I think I heard Mr. Miller call him Jet? But I'm not sure. The man drinks like a fish, so who knows what he was mumbling." Horace straightened.

I nodded, casting a smile at him. "Interesting." I let each syllable slowly roll off my tongue.

Suddenly, Horace's gaze was back on me. His eyebrows were knit together, and his tight shoulders had returned. "Stay away from them, Ms. Livingstone. They are not good people. That whole family is mixed up in some bad stuff."

My pulse began to pound as I shrugged, hoping he'd think I wasn't interested in Jet, and I slunk back to the part of the wall I'd been holding up.

I watched as Jet helped his father hobble over to the columns in front of the hotel. Mr. Miller reached out to lean against one.

The valet looked disgruntled as he studied the two of them. I wondered if he was going to say something, but when a black Jaguar pulled up, the valet sprang into action. A few seconds later, Mr. Miller straightened as he began yelling at Jet.

After a few violent waves of his hand that almost caused

him to topple over, Mr. Miller half-walked, half-stumbled away from the front and around the corner, disappearing from view.

My gaze made its way back to Jet, who was standing there, watching his dad leave. His brows were knit together, and his eyes narrowed. I recognized the look of disappointment written all over his face. It was one I'd had on very many occasions for my own parental units.

When it became apparent that his dad wasn't going to return, Jet shoved his hands into the pockets of his jacket and dipped his head. He made his way down the sidewalk, and just before he disappeared, he turned and met my gaze again.

Heat pricked my cheeks as I contemplated looking away —I didn't want him to know I'd been watching him—but I couldn't bring myself to do it. It felt as if there was something stopping me from moving...breathing...anything.

Thankfully, it only lasted a few seconds before he lowered his gaze and disappeared around the corner.

My heart was racing at a pace that made me grateful for ribcages. I was pretty sure it would have taken off if not confined.

I leaned against the wall and tipped my head back, closing my eyes. I could see the depth of his stare and the hurt in his gaze as he studied me. And all I could do was stare at him. Maybe Kate knew him. I was going to have to call her later and ask.

And then I felt like a stalker. Great.

I was such a loser.

"Brielle Livingstone, what are you doing out here?"

Nothing like good ole Mom to snap me back to reality. I straightened and glanced over to see her approach with a very disgruntled expression. As she drew near, she wrapped her hand around my arm and pulled me closer.

"I'm sorry, Mom," I said as I allowed her to drag me back toward the restaurant. "I just don't want to be a part of whatever you and Dad are conspiring."

Mom's gaze slipped over to me and she sighed. "You are a Livingstone. It's your responsibility to make sure the name lives on." She hesitated and brought me closer to her. "Whatever we ask of you, we expect you to obey." She met my gaze. "You understand that, right?"

Why did I feel like Mom was asking me to give away my firstborn? Did what I want matter to them at all?

Before I allowed that question to reach my lips, I let out a sigh and nodded. Truth was, my parents didn't care about me. They didn't care about how I felt. They had a mission, and, no matter what or who they hurt, they were going to accomplish it.

"Of course," I whispered as I forced a fake smile.

Mom's wrinkles relaxed as the first genuine smile I'd seen in a long time played on her lips. She pulled me into a hug that felt like an attempt at closeness.

"I knew I could depend on you," she said as she held me for a moment.

I nodded as I followed after her and obediently sat down in my vacated chair. Stefano smiled over at me, and I returned it.

It didn't matter how I felt about this or what my parents were about to ask me to do. Mom had said it perfectly. I was a Livingstone. It was my job, and I was going to do it no matter how much I didn't want to.

It was my birthright. I had no choice.

CHAPTER THREE

The lunch progressed with very boring conversation. Stefano kept trying to engage me in small talk. First it was about the weather, then about a sports team. When I mistakenly called a football touchdown a goal, the frustration in Stefano's voice and hand gestures became grossly apparent, so I decided silence was probably best.

And with neither of us talking, I could hear what my parents were plotting on the other end of the table. It was right around the time I heard Mom say, "they'll have such a fun time," that I decided they needed my full attention.

"I'm sorry, what?" I asked as I turned and shot Mom a death stare.

Mom, of course, didn't respond. Instead, she smiled at Mr. Esposito and waved me off. "Oh, Brielle. You'll get used to her special brand of humor." She reached under the table and squeezed my leg.

I yelped, which caused her to loosen her grip. Stefano gave me a confused look, but I just smiled it away. "I'm sorry, what does that mean? He'll get used to it?"

"You're coming to Italy for the summer, and maybe longer," Stefano said as he leaned in and wiggled his eyebrows. "You know this, right?" He stuck his spoon into a large scoop of gelato.

I stared at him. "I'm sorry…what?"

Mom sighed. "Don't be dramatic," she hissed as she leaned in. Her breath was hot on my ear.

"I'm going to Italy for the summer?" I asked, pulling away. I wasn't in the mood for her *don't cause a scene* lecture. My parents were shipping me off to some foreign country with people I didn't even know. "Why?"

Gah. I hated how my voice came out all high-pitched and scratchy. Like I had no control over my emotions— which I didn't, but I didn't want them to know that.

"It will be fun," Mom said, giving me a wide smile.

I stared at her. So, she wasn't even going to pretend that what I'd just heard was a lie. Which meant…

My lungs began to constrict as my eyesight blurred. The walls in this ridiculously enormous hotel felt as if they were closing in on me. My breath came out in short, staccato bursts. I needed to get out of here. And not just to the foyer.

Out of here, out of here.

I stumbled to my feet. I was pretty sure Mom said something to me, but I couldn't make it out. My whole head felt as if I were underwater—everything looked blurry and sounded muffled.

All I could think about was how much I needed some air.

Mom made a grab for me, but I didn't care. I lifted my arm and broke her grip.

Somehow, I made it out of the dining room, through the kitchen, and out to the back alley. As soon as the salty, warm outside air filled my lungs, my mind began to clear.

I tipped my head up to the sky and let the warmth of the sun wash over me.

After a few very deep breaths, I began to feel a tad ridiculous for reacting the way I had. I mean, who wouldn't want to spend their summer in Italy, laying on the beaches and eating pasta. But I knew it wouldn't be a dream vacation. With my parents, it never was.

It was going to be a nightmare, and I would be stuck in it. At least here there was some semblance of freedom. There, I wouldn't have any friends, speak the language, or know which side of the road to drive on.

"That was incredibly rude," Mom's high-pitched and very annoyed voice drew my attention.

I groaned, making sure it was loud and very obnoxious. I wanted her to know how much I hated what she and Dad were doing to me. The fact that they were planning my summer—my future—without my consent was not okay.

"Mom, what is going on? Why did Stefano say that I was going to spend my summer—the summer before my senior year—in Italy with him?"

Mom's cheeks were flushed with frustration as she eyed

me. "What? I thought you'd be excited to spend summer vacation in a foreign country."

I shook my head. "If I was there with Kate or Betty, sure. Not with some foreign rich kid who you obviously have plans for." I studied Mom, waiting for her telltale sign that she was up to no good.

Mom stared at me, and. just when I thought she wasn't going to, her right eye twitched. Bingo. I was right.

I groaned again and folded my arms across my chest. "Why? Why are you sending me away? What could that possibly bring to the family?"

Plus, I was terrified of planes. Just thinking about how long I would be stuck in one with Stefano made me want to check myself into a mental institution. Was what she was gaining worth losing her only daughter?

Probably.

Mom pinched her lips together and then let her breath out slowly. "There are some sacrifices we have to make in this family, Brielle. You have to accept this." She fiddled with her extremely tight braid at the nape of her neck. "We expect you to be ready by Monday to spend the summer with the Espositos and Stefano. We expect you to be sweet and respectful. A merger of our families would only strengthen the Livingstone name." She narrowed her eyes as she studied me, like I was supposed to understand what that meant.

Which, unfortunately, I did. I was spoken for. It was our parents' intention to get me and Stefano together. To get married. I wouldn't screw over my own family, and that's what my parents were banking on.

I was suddenly shoved about two hundred years into the past, where my parents were arranging my marriage and telling me who I could love.

Instead of answering her, I just turned away. I was too hurt and way too mad to respond. I didn't want to hear how I needed take my role in this family seriously. I also didn't need to hear Mom tell me that it would be all right and that I was just overreacting.

But most of all, I didn't want Mom to see the tears brimming on the edge of my eyelids. I was pretty sure that in mere seconds, the waterworks were going to spill.

Mom let out a frustrated sigh, and I didn't need to look to know that her stern expression had turned to one of annoyance. She was staring at her blubbering daughter, whose reaction was only going to inconvenience her. She couldn't understand how I always let my emotions get the better of me.

But I couldn't pretend everything was alright. I was a wreck inside.

"I'm going back in to finish lunch. Take the time you need, but I expect you back in your room in a few hours. You are taking Stefano out this afternoon and showing him the highlights of Atlantic City."

I kept my head ducked down as I nodded. I didn't have the energy to fight her anymore. She'd made up her mind, and experience had taught me that there was no changing it.

I heard her footsteps pause near me, and she reached out

her hand to very awkwardly pat me on the back. I wanted to pull away, but I stayed there, hiding from the world as the sound of her footsteps grew quieter until they disappeared.

I stood there for a few minutes as I tried to gather my thoughts. I didn't want to look like a blubbering idiot as I walked around the hotel. I wasn't going to move away from the safety of the alley until I had my emotions under control.

But the more I thought about what had happened, the madder I got. Who did Dad and Mom think they were? Selling me off to the highest bidder and expecting that I would just go along with it.

What the heck? I was almost an adult. I didn't have to stand by and take this. They were the ones who needed to seal this deal, not me. They were going to have to find a way that didn't include me.

"Ridiculous," I breathed out as I pushed away from the wall and made my way around the corner of the building. Dumpsters were lined up against the wall. I pinched the bridge of my nose as I studied the ground. I just needed to figure out how to get out of this.

"Is this what a nervous breakdown looks like?" a deep, mocking voice asked me.

I closed my eyes for a moment. I really wasn't up for dealing with some half-drunk, gambling-crazed man right now. "Can you just leave me alone?" I asked. I spun toward the voice, only to practically swallow my tongue.

Jet Miller was leaning against the building with his legs stretched out in front of him and a half-cocked smile on his face. He reached up and pulled earbuds from his ears. He had a pocketknife in his hand, and he returned to whittling the stick he was holding in his other hand.

"What?" he asked as he slid the knife down the branch, shards flying everywhere.

Was this like a hobby for him? It didn't seem to match his personality. And then I felt dumb. He was probably sharpening his knife for his next fight, not carving masterpieces out of wood.

His gaze held mine as his eyebrows rose. Almost like he was waiting for me to say something.

Right. Talking. I knew how to do that.

"Nervous breakdown? No. Panic attack? Yes." Heat instantly rushed to my cheeks. Why was I talking like a robot? "I mean..."

No words came to my mind. Literally all the words I knew flew out, leaving an empty space between my ears.

Instead of standing there like a blubbering fish, I pinched my lips shut—Mom would be so proud—and returned to pacing.

Jet didn't seem phased by my brain spasm and returned to running his blade across the wood, sending shavings everywhere.

"What does a girl like you have to panic about?"

There was a hint of distain to his voice that caused me to pause. It was almost like he didn't like me. Which was stupid. We'd literally never met before.

"Excuse me?" I asked before I could stop myself. Was he joking? And then I suddenly realized that there was a very good chance that he'd heard everything that just went down with my mom and me. I mean, was he even listening to anything on those earbuds, or was he just wearing them so he could collect people's secrets?

"Eavesdrop much?" I snapped back at him. As the words left my lips, regret filled my stomach. I didn't mean to take my anger out on him. But I was embarrassed, and the fact that he'd stood in the shadows and overheard me and Mom, well, that frustrated me.

My messed-up family life was mine. It wasn't something I wanted to share with total strangers. No matter how much my body warmed from his widening smile.

Jet flicked his gaze up to me before returning it to his stick. "Hey, I was here first. Not my fault you decided to air your dirty laundry in front of an audience." Then he chuckled. He lifted his hand, still clutching the knife, and motioned toward his headphones. "But don't worry, I didn't hear a thing. Music." He shrugged. "I doubt it would matter anyway. You rich people know how to keep your secrets."

I scoffed. It escaped before I could stop it. But that was the best comeback I could come up with. I was exhausted.

Suddenly feeling like I might pass out, I moved to lean against the bit of wall beside him. I would have picked another spot, but there were dumpsters on either side of us.

I bent my knees and rested my hands on my legs. I took a few deep breaths and didn't feel any better. It either had to do with the fact that Jet was inches away from me or that the fight with Mom was still reeling in my mind.

Hopefully it was the latter.

"We all have messed up families," Jet said, like that was supposed to make me feel better.

I glanced over at him. He was studying the stick as he turned it from side to side. He settled on a new spot and started scraping it.

Annoyance nipped at me. "What are you doing here? Can't you do that"—I waved at his hands—"somewhere else?"

Jet glanced over at me as he continued scraping. "Don't you know that this particular spot gets the best sunlight in this whole town?" He pointed toward the sky, and, like an idiot, I followed his finger.

It only took a second for Jet to snort and for me to realize that I looked like a complete idiot. I glared at him as I pushed off the wall. I'd brave my nausea if it meant I didn't have to stand next to him anymore.

"Har har," I said as I folded my arms. But my curiosity was winning out. Why hadn't he gone home after his dad had been thrown out?

"Trouble in paradise?" I asked and then felt stupid for phrasing it that way. "I mean..."

I forgot what I was saying when he glanced up.

His eyes had turned stormy and his eyebrows furrowed. I had a sinking feeling it had to do with his family and what I had implied. He straightened and chucked the stick into a nearby dumpster.

"I'm sorry," I said as I stepped closer to him. "I didn't mean..."

"Listen, Blondie, you don't know me and I don't know

you. I don't belong in your world and you don't belong in mine." He folded his knife and slipped it into his front pocket. "Let's not pretend like we come from the same place or that you know anything about me."

My lips parted as I watched him push the hair that had fallen across his forehead to the side and then shove both hands into his pockets.

I hadn't meant to upset him. I was just frustrated that he was making snap judgements about me, and I couldn't help but do the same back.

Before either of us could speak, a deep voice sounded behind us. "Who's back here?" it growled.

I sighed. It was probably Horace or one of his goons out patrolling for me. I stepped forward to call out to them, but Jet jumped into my line of sight and pulled me over until my back was against the wall. I was caged between his arms.

Confused, I glanced up to see him staring down at me with a begging hint to his gaze.

"I said, who's back here?" the man grumbled again. His voice was growing louder.

I glanced over Jet's shoulder and then back up to him, only to find that he was leaning closer. He was so close that our lips were mere inches apart. His chest was so close to mine that I could feel the warmth emanating from his body. I knew I should have at least been concerned about him basically pinning me to the wall, but I wasn't.

"Go with me on this," he whispered as he brought his lips closer to mine.

My heart was racing, and my breathing had turned shallow. For some inane reason, I wanted him to close the gap. Call it rebellion. Call it wanting to be kissed by the cutest guy in Atlantic City. I just wanted him to do it.

I raised my gaze to his only to find him studying me. His brows were knit together as his gaze kept slipping down to my lips.

"What are we doing?" I asked, my voice low and breathy.

Jet parted his lips to speak but was interrupted when the man bellowed, "Hey, what are you two doing?"

Before I could glance behind Jet to see who was standing there, he closed the gap in one swift movement. His lips brushed mine, and all thought flew from my mind.

A warm sensation rushed across my skin and exploded through my body. I was too stunned to do anything. I wanted to move, but I couldn't. Everything about Jet was intoxicating me, from the woody scent of his cologne to the softness of his lips that fit perfectly against mine.

"Get out of here," the man yelled.

Jet pulled away but kept his face ducked down. "Sorry, sir," he said.

"This isn't a make-out spot. It's a business. Get out of here before I call the police."

Jet reached down and grabbed my hand. "Hide your face," he said as he pulled me alongside him.

We kept our heads down as we skirted past the guard and made our way through the alley to the street. He led me around the corner, where he dropped my hand and turned, smiling over at me.

My brain had finally caught up with my surroundings.

Still not one hundred percent sure what was going on, I studied him.

"Thanks," he said as he made his way over to a black motorcycle and grabbed the helmet off the back.

I forced my legs to move as I hurried after him. "What was that?" I asked. My voice came out shaky and unsure. I swallowed hard, hoping to still my nerves.

"You were my getaway car," he said as he slipped his helmet on and grinned down at me.

Anger coursed through my veins as I stared at him. "What?" I managed.

Jet buckled the strap under his chin. "There was no way that guard would have let me go if it weren't for you. So, thanks." He winked as he slung his leg over his bike and pulled it off the kickstand.

I was still trying to figure out what had happened as he pulled his key from his pocket and slipped it in the ignition. I grabbed the handles.

"Where are you going?" I asked. Or more like demanded. There was no way he was slipping out of here after pulling something like that.

Jet stared at me. "I've gotta go. If you can't tell, I'm not welcome around here. Now, will you kindly move?"

I gripped harder on the bars. Call me crazy, but I was tired of people using me for their own gain. It was time someone helped *me* for a change. "No."

His eyebrows rose. "No?"

I steadied my feet as I stared him down. "You don't just get to kiss me and then leave. I'm not that kind of girl."

He leaned forward, his forearms resting on my hands. "You're not?"

I scowled at him. "No. And because I helped you out, I expect something in exchange."

He leaned back and folded his arms across his chest. "You do?"

Feeling more confident than I had in a very long time, I smiled. "Yes."

"And what do you want?"

I swallowed. The words I wanted to say stuck in the back of my throat. Not only because he was a complete stranger, but also because it was going to tick my parents off. More than anything else I'd ever done.

But I needed freedom. I needed to get out of the stifling world my parents created for me. I forced all the courage I could muster together and said, "Take me with you."

CHAPTER FOUR

The laugh that escaped Jet's lips only fueled my frustration. He twisted the front of his motorcycle to try to break my grip. I only held on tighter.

"You're crazy," he said as he glanced over at me. "I can't take you with me. Your parents would call the police. And then what?" He studied me and shook his head.

I stepped closer. I needed this. For all I knew, my parents were shipping me off to Italy in two days. There was no way I could spend the weekend playing hostess to the family that would take me away. I needed to live.

"Please?" I asked, hoping my puppy dog eyes were enough to convince him.

Jet studied me but shook his head. "I don't even know your name, and you don't know mine. What if I'm a serial killer?"

Right. He didn't know that I knew who he was. I was

grateful that I hadn't let it slip before now. The last thing I needed was him reading into the fact that I'd been asking Horace about him.

"I'm Brielle, and you're...?" I nodded toward him.

He narrowed his eyes. "I'm not telling you. Then we'd be acquaintances." He turned the key and the motorcycle roared to life. "I'm leaving," he shouted over the rumble of the engine.

I leaned closer to him so he could hear me. "I'll pay you," I said. He had to need money. Money always got people to do things. Just ask my parents.

That seemed to get through to him because he idled the engine as he stared at me.

"How much?"

My heart began to pound inside of my chest. Maybe a part of me had been convinced there was no way I could get him to agree. Now that I was close, adrenaline was rushing through me. "A thousand for the weekend."

His lips parted as he stared at me. Then he scoffed as he killed the engine. "There's no way you have that kind of money."

I pinched my lips together. It would be difficult, but I had an account set up for me by my grandparents. Technically it was for college, but what did that matter anymore? I was apparently a child bride. I doubted Mr. Italian wanted his betrothed to go to school.

"My parents own the Livingstone hotels." I leaned closer. "I can get the money."

He let go of the handles as he leaned back. He folded one arm across his chest and rested his other elbow on his hand. "What do you mean weekend? How long do you want to tag along with me?"

I chewed my lip. My mind was racing a mile a minute. The thought that I might have some freedom from my controlling parents was doing strange things to my insides.

"As long as I can. Take me somewhere. Show me parts of Atlantic City that I've never been to." I shrugged like it was no big deal. I'd spent most of my summers here, and yet, I hadn't done much. I was always at the hotel, doing daughter duties. If I was about to head across the ocean, I wanted to experience everything.

Jet snorted. "Okay. I'm not sure what I can show you. My world is different than yours."

I shook my head. "Stop saying that. We're not that different."

"Right."

The air fell silent around us as I stared at him. I wanted him to say yes. I was willing it.

He met my gaze and then sighed. "Fine." He nodded toward the back of his bike. "Get on."

My knees almost buckled as I stared at his bike. For some reason, I hadn't thought about actually riding on it. Man, I was an idiot sometimes. "We're going on that?"

Jet glanced over at me. "Yeah. It's my only ride." Then he moved to unbuckle his helmet. "Here," he said as he shoved it into my hands.

I took it, still not sure if I was totally on board with this. "Is it safe?" I glanced up at him. "How do I know you're not going to knock me off after you get my money?"

Jet scoffed. Then he shrugged. "Not going to lie. That crossed my mind." He gave me a teasing smile. I glared at him.

He sighed. "You're just going to have to trust me. Or don't come. I don't really care."

"You promise me that you're not going to ditch me the first chance you get?"

He raised his hand like he was swearing in court.

"And you promise that you won't kill me on that thing?"

He groaned. "It's the only way I'm going to be able to get you from point a to point b." He started up the engine again. "But, yes, I promise not to kill you."

I pinched my lips together as I stared at the back of the bike. I could do this. I could totally do this. Right?

"Make your decision, Blondie. I can't wait forever."

"Brielle," I said as I slipped the helmet over my head and secured it. A thrill rushed through me as I stepped closer to him. I was actually going to do this. My head felt light as I forced my nerves to calm.

"Right. Blondie—Brielle. They sound the same to me." He laughed.

I wasn't sure how to climb onto a motorcycle in a dress, so I held onto his shoulders as I swung a leg over and sat, tucking my dress under my legs to keep it from flying up.

Once I was pretty sure I wasn't going to flash anyone, I

focused back on Jet. My heart pounded as I stared at his leather-clad back. I hadn't noticed until this moment how broad his shoulders were, and I hadn't anticipated how small I would feel pressed up next to him.

He glanced over his shoulder, and his cocky smile softened as he studied me. "You okay?"

The butterflies inside of my stomach felt like missiles as they dive-bombed at lightning speed. "Yes," I whispered.

He revved the engine as he nodded toward me. "You'll want to hold on. Don't want to lose you before we get to the bank."

"We're going there right now?" I yelled over the roaring engine.

"Yep. I've got trust issues, and I don't work for free."

I chewed the inside of my cheek as I nodded. "Of course. Right."

"Are you ready?"

I wrapped my arms around his waist, pulling my body closer to his. His cologne filled my nostrils. My hands were pressed into his abs and I was trying really hard to ignore the fact that I could practically feel every muscle. "Yes," I whispered.

"Yes?"

I nodded into his back.

"Perfect." He pushed the kickstand up and turned back at me. "Name's Jet."

I nodded again but didn't look up. Maybe it was fear. Maybe it was the fact that this was easily the most rebellious thing I'd done in my whole life, but I needed him to get moving before I lost my nerve.

Thankfully, Jet wasn't bothered by my silence, and he pulled away from the curb.

At first, I felt like I was going to throw up. My stomach was in knots. and the rush of the world around me made me disoriented. I couldn't be sick. I'd never live that down.

So I said a little prayer, and a few minutes later, my stomach settled, and I could actually pull my head away from Jet's back and look around.

It was strange, seeing Atlantic City like this. I'd always been in a car when traveling through the city, and my parents weren't much for rolling the windows down.

But here, on the back of Jet's bike, it was like I was seeing this city for the first time.

The ocean peeked out every so often between the large, looming hotels. Places that my father intended on purchasing. He often talked about taking over Atlantic City. That it was somehow my destiny. A destiny that I didn't want and would never pick for myself.

But they wouldn't listen to me. They never would.

Anger boiled up inside of me, so I pushed my parents from my mind. That wasn't what this weekend was about. It was my last hurrah before I went home and faced whatever my parents had planned for me.

But for now, this was about me. All about me. And I was going to enjoy every minute of it.

It didn't take long for Jet to pull up in front of the bank.

He nodded toward the doors and raised his fingers, rubbing them together.

I rolled my eyes as I climbed off the motorcycle. The freezing cold air caused me to shiver as I stepped into the lobby. A woman with a bubbly smile nodded at me, indicating that I could step up to her window.

"How can I help you, sweetheart?" she asked in a full-on southern drawl.

I turned and pulled my debit card from my bra. "I need to make a withdrawal from my account," I said as I slid the card across the counter. "Name's Brielle Livingstone, and my pin is 8569."

The woman took it and nodded. "Fingerprint," she said, motioning toward a small black box off to the side.

I complied, and it must have worked because she said, "How much are you looking to take out?"

I fiddled with a pen that was attached to a chain. "A grand."

Her gaze snapped over to me. "A thousand?"

I nodded.

She clicked her tongue as she stared at her screen. For a moment, I wondered if she was going to say something. But she pulled open her drawer. "What kind of bills would you like, sweetie?"

I breathed a sigh of relief. "Twenties are fine."

She counted them out in front of me, and I nodded along with her. When all fifty bills were laid out, she grabbed an envelope, stacked the bills, and slipped them inside. Then she handed the pile over to me.

"Here you go, Ms. Livingstone. Is there anything else I can help you with today?"

I shook my head as I clutched the envelope in my hand. "Nope. I'm good. Thanks."

"You have a nice day then."

I smiled over at her as I turned and made my way through the bank. I half-expected to find Jet gone when I stepped outside, so I was pleasantly surprised to see him sitting on his bike right where I had left him. His gaze roamed over me, and I held up the envelope as I walked over to him.

I opened it and pulled out a handful of twenties. He protested, but I shook my head.

"Half now. Half later," I said as I pulled the other half out of the envelope and folded it then slipped it into my bra.

My skin heated as Jet's eyebrows went up. He didn't hide the fact that he'd watched me stash the money. I shrugged. "Purses ruin my outfit," I said as I grabbed the helmet and slipped it over my head.

Jet chuckled as he pulled the motorcycle off its kick-stand. "I didn't say anything."

I wrapped my arms around his waist. "But you were thinking it."

The roar of the motorcycle drowned out his laugh as he stuck out his left hand and merged into traffic.

The farther we got from Livingstone Hotel, the freer I felt. It was liberating, putting Mom and Dad in the rearview mirror. Even though, in the back of my mind, I knew it was for only a short time, I was going to enjoy it. My last weekend of freedom before I succumbed to my parent's insanity and followed my destiny to sign my soul over to the highest bidder.

I deserved this break.

It didn't take long before Jet was pulling into a parking lot that lined the beach. Nice thing about a motorcycle, you can literally park anywhere. Once the engine was off, I moved to dismount only to find Jet's hand appear from over his shoulder. Like he was trying to assist.

"Thanks," I mumbled as I allowed him to help me down.

I stood there, feeling like an idiot as Jet chuckled and pushed the kickstand down.

"You're an investment," he said. "I wouldn't want you to trip and call this whole thing off." He swung his leg off the motorcycle and straightened.

My heart literally skipped a beat as I glanced up to take in his full six-foot-something frame. His leather jacket clung to his body, hinting to the muscle underneath.

To say he was formidable looking, standing there in front of me, was an understatement.

"You okay?" he asked as he reached up to help with my helmet.

The warmth of his fingers and how they lightly danced over my skin sent shivers down my back. I jumped back, startled from the way his touch affected me.

"I've got it," I said as I reached up to unclasp the chin strap.

Jet raised his hands as a slow, sly smile emerged. "You looked like you were in a trance. I was just helping you out."

I slipped the helmet off and handed it over. He turned to set the helmet on his bike, which gave me a moment to rub away the feeling of his fingers against my neck. I was pretty sure my cheeks were burning red.

I really needed to get a grip if I was going to be able to handle this weekend. Or else Jet would realize that he'd agreed to help a crazy person and drop me back off at the hotel.

When he turned, his relaxed smile helped put my nerves at ease. He looked calm. Which was strange. He'd been so broody before. He was a mystery that I wanted to figure out.

"Ready?" he asked, nodding toward the ocean.

I glanced where he'd motioned and then back to him. "The water? Seriously?"

He shrugged. "The boardwalk. It leads to the pier."

"Pier?"

His jaw dropped. "Yeah. Steel Pier. How long have you lived in Atlantic City?"

I shrugged as I followed after him. His stride was about double mine, so I had to rush to keep up. "Since I was seven. But I spend most of my time in New York."

Jet glanced over at me. "New York? Why?"

"I go to a prep school there. Although I suspect that my parents send me there so I don't get in their way." I pulled my fingers through my curls and secured my hair in a ponytail at the nape of my neck.

"Your parents sound like winners," he said as he slipped his hands into his leather jacket and glanced over at me.

"They're okay. I mean, I know they care about me. They just have a weird way of showing it."

Jet chuckled as he kicked a rock, sending it shooting across the sand.

I peeked over at him, wondering about his dad. I wasn't sure how to ask him about what had happened at the hotel earlier, so I decided to take a less direct route.

"What about you?"

"Me?"

"Yeah. Any parental drama going on in your world?"

When he grew quiet, I worried I'd somehow offended him. But I wasn't sure how I could have. We were talking about parents; the most logical step was for him to share his own experience.

"I really don't want to talk about them," he said.

I nodded—probably a bit too vigorously. "I get it. No worries." I bit down on my tongue, stopping myself from saying anything more.

He was studying me when I turned my attention to him. His eyebrow was quirked as he watched me.

Suddenly self-conscious, I patted down my hair and rubbed my face. "What?" I asked when I couldn't feel anything out of place.

He just shrugged. "Nothing," he said as he quickened his pace, making me triple my stride to keep up with him.

Irritated, I reached out and grabbed his arm. "Hey," I said as I attempted to pull him to a stop. "If you keep walking like this, you're going to wear me out."

He laughed as he slowed his gait. "Maybe that's a good thing?"

I shook my head. "You're not getting rid of me that fast. I'm paying for a weekend, so I expect a weekend."

He nodded as his smile softened. "And you're not worried your parents are going to come looking for you?"

My stomach hitched. Truth was, I was pretty certain that Mom and Dad were going to have a search party out scouring the city for me by nightfall—but I didn't care. It wasn't like I was a kid anymore.

I bolstered my courage and shook my head. "I'm a rebel. They need to get used to that."

Jet paused, while I kept walking. When I noticed, I stopped and turned to see him run his gaze over me. He snorted.

"Sure you are," he said as he passed by me.

Frustrated, I moved to keep up with him. "What does that mean?"

He paused and stared down at me. My brain must have short-circuited, because I stopped moving as well. It wasn't until he leaned in that I realized how close we were.

My gaze involuntarily dipped down to his lips. The memory of kissing him rushed back to me and caused my whole body to heat. It was like one of those moments where you're not sure if you dreamed it or if it was real. My mind was saying it had happened, but the logical part of my brain was telling me I'd dreamed it.

I wanted to kiss him again just to prove to myself that it had happened.

"Brielle Livingstone, I doubt you could ever really be a rebel," he said, snapping me back to reality, despite the fact that my mind was still swimming.

Before I could retort, he turned and headed toward the ticket counter.

I stared after him as his words sunk in. That wasn't true, was it?

CHAPTER FIVE

*L*uckily, Jet's conversation with the ticket teller saved him from my frustration. I didn't want to broach the topic while he was chatting—probably flirting—with the girl behind the counter.

After he paid, he handed me my ticket and extended his hand for me to follow. When we entered the park, I turned to him with determination. He was going to hear just how rebellious I really was.

"Oh no," he said as he stared down at me with a teasing smile on his lips. "What's wrong?"

I studied him, frustrated that in one movement he could still my rage. The sparkle in his eye told me he knew what he was doing. He was trying to get me all worked up.

I glared at him as I shook my head. "That's not fair," I said, stomping over to get in line at the mini doughnut shop.

Jet followed me and leaned in. "What's not fair?"

My body warmed from his presence. That both irritated and excited me. But there was no way I wanted him to discover that, so I turned and glared at him. "You know my drama, and yet, I don't know yours."

His expression stilled as he straightened. His tanned skin blushed as he cleared his throat. "You don't want to know, Blondie."

Great. Back to that nickname. I watched as he stared at the prices above the counter. He had no interest in what a dozen mini doughnuts cost; he was avoiding talking to me. Or looking me in my eye.

"Why do you say that?" I asked, feeling brave enough to goad him a bit. He was using what he knew about my family against me, it was only fair that I know something about him—other than that his father was thrown out of the casino.

He had to know that I knew about his dad. I mean, he'd looked right at me when he left. But, I could be wrong.

"Do you suffer from short-term memory loss?" I asked.

His brows furrowed. "No. Why?"

I shrugged as I moved forward in the line. "No reason. Just trying to figure you out." I pretended like I was ticking thoughts off on the tip of my fingers. "I'm guessing since you can ride a motorcycle, you don't have some sort of far-off blindness." I scrunched my nose.

Jet stared at me like I had two heads. "What are you talking about?"

Sighing, I shook my head. He really didn't want to talk to

me about himself. It kind of hurt that he was being so secretive. "Never mind," I said.

Jet shoved his hands into the front of his jeans and shrugged his shoulders. "My family's a mess. Not something that you want to get mixed up in."

I studied him. For a moment, it felt as if Jet Miller was being vulnerable. It was probably the truest thing he'd said to me since I met him. It didn't take a genius to see that his family had issues. But whose family was perfect? Certainly not mine.

I gave him a small smile. "Wow. That's...deep."

He scrunched up his face as he mocked a hurt look. "Thanks," he said as he scoffed and nodded behind me. "Your turn," he said.

I glanced behind me to see that I was next in line. After ordering a dozen mini doughnuts, I stepped off to the side to wait for them to come out of the fryer. I folded my arms and leaned against the outside of the small building, hoping that we could move our conversation away from our families.

"So, do you go to school around here?"

Jet glanced over at me. "I actually just graduated."

I raised my eyebrows. "Wow. So, summer before college?"

Jet shook his head. "Not really. Summer before work is more like it." He reached up and pushed his hand through his hair. "Dad says it's time I take responsibility for the family."

The way he said the words made me wonder if he hadn't

meant for me to hear that. They came out soft, sort of like a thought escaping his lips unbidden.

I studied him, wondering what he could mean. His parents wanted him to take responsibility? It made me wonder if this leather-wearing, motorcycle-riding guy and I actually had something in common.

Did he also know what soul-crushing family responsibility felt like?

His cheeks flushed as he glanced over to me. He cleared his throat.

"Anyway. Didn't mean to bring you into my mess." He nodded toward my bag of mini doughnuts. "How do those taste?"

I slipped one into my mouth and then licked the sugar off my fingertips. "Divine." I tipped the bag toward him. "Want one?"

He glanced over at me and then back to the bag. He shrugged as he pulled one out and popped it into his mouth. "Wow," he said as his lips curled around his teeth as if to hold in the sugar. "Those are good."

I nodded as I pulled out another doughnut. "Cinnamon sugar makes everything better," I said as we passed through the entrance of the pier and into the amusement park.

Families were moving around us. Kids shouted with excitement as they ran from one side of the pier to another. I felt a tad old as I studied the kiddie rides that lined the edges.

"Are we too old for this place?" I asked, glancing over at him.

Jet shrugged. "Eh, age is just a number, right?"

I stared at the ride with tiny airplanes affixed to it. "Yeah, I don't think age matters in the case of your giant-ness and these tiny rides."

Jet scoffed. "Are you calling me fat?"

He said that at the same moment I slipped a doughnut into my mouth. I tried to laugh, but cinnamon sugar shot to the back of my throat and threw me into a coughing fit.

Jet's eyebrows rose, but I waved him away. Embarrassment coursed through my body as my eyes watered.

"You okay?" he asked, reaching out to whack my back.

"Yeah. I'm good," I wheezed.

Wow. How ladylike was I being right now? I'm sure I looked so incredibly sexy standing on this pier, hacking up a lung. Thankfully, it didn't take long for my coughing to subside to a dull ache in the back of my throat.

I swallowed a few times, hoping to erase the rawness that had settled there.

"Be careful," he said as he studied me.

"Yeah. Will do." There were only a few doughnuts left in the bottom of the bag, so to save my throat and my dignity, I threw them into a nearby garbage.

I brushed off my hands and turned to smile at him. "I thought it wise," I said, nodding toward the trash.

"Probably smart," he said.

We stood in silence for a few seconds before he sighed. "Shall we?"

I glanced over to see him motion toward the Ferris wheel. "Really?"

He shrugged. "Unless you want to try fitting on the airplane ride."

I snorted as I quickened my pace toward the giant spinning wheel. When we got to the ticket taker, Jet handed him the tickets and we waited until the wheel stopped moving and the attendant slid open the bar so we could board the ride.

Once we were seated, the attendant latched the door, and we were off.

I clung to the edge of the seat as the clouds came into view, our bucket climbing high into the sky. I tried not to look down and wonder how it would feel to plummet to the ground.

"Do you not like heights?" Jet asked.

I turned and pinched my lips together as I shook my head. "Not really. But I'm trying to get over it. I'm tired of taking sleeping medicine every time I get on a plane."

Jet leaned back against his seat and stretched out his legs. They brushed against mine, sending shivers across my skin. I contemplated moving, but when Jet didn't budge, I decided to let it go.

Was it wrong if I liked it?

"Do you do a lot of flying?"

I glanced over at him. He looked genuinely interested in my answer.

"Yeah. To New York and back. My mom likes to travel, and sometimes she takes me with." I couldn't help the sadness that coated my tone as I stared at the ocean that stretched out in front of us.

There had been moments in my life when Mom wasn't crazy. When she wasn't trying to turn me into an olden-day bride. She could be cool and relaxed if she wanted to be. But most of the time she was a bundle of raw nerves.

"Sounds like fun," Jet said.

I glanced over at him. There was a sadness in his voice that made me wonder.

"Not much of a traveler?" I asked as I clasped my hands together and squeezed them. I needed something more to do than just sit there and stare at him.

Jet shrugged as he extended his arm to rest on the back of his seat. "No. Didn't ever have the money." He sighed, blowing out his breath in one long motion. "Hard to when Dad's a drunk and Mom's working minimum wage."

Ah. Finally, I was learning a bit more about Jet. It was like a puzzle that I was anxious to put together. Who he was and where he came from. I wanted to know everything.

I must have waited too long to respond because when I parted my lips to say something, Jet just shrugged and leaned forward, resting his elbows on his knees.

"Sorry," he said as he brought his gaze up to meet mine. "I don't know why my thoughts are like a faucet around you." He sighed as he leaned back. "Didn't think you'd be getting involved with a guy who was a giant mess, did you?"

I shrugged. I didn't want him to think that I wasn't enjoying him opening up to me.

"It's nice...you know." I took a deep breath. "Knowing that I'm not the only one with crazy parents. Or life problems."

His chuckle was soft as he shook his head. "You have problems? How?"

For some reason, it hurt that he thought I had everything made. As if a girl with wealthy parents couldn't possibly feel alone or frustrated. Or want a different life for herself, even if her parents were determined that her life was going in the direction they thought best.

It was like I was stuck, frozen by my parents' expectations. And Jet just writing all that off made me...mad. I wasn't the spoiled girl that he was painting me to be.

When I didn't respond, Jet glanced over at me. His gaze roamed over my face, and for a moment, I saw regret flash in his eyes.

"Sorry, Brielle. I didn't mean..." He blew out his breath as he scrubbed his face. "I can be a jerk sometimes."

Not wanting to show him how much he'd hurt me, I shrugged as I wrapped my arms around my chest. "It's okay," I whispered.

He studied me and then cursed under his breath. "Let's make a pact. I won't ask you about your family, and you won't ask me about mine. There are some things that should just be secret." He held out his hand. "Deal?"

I wasn't a fan of that idea, but if it kept the conversation light and easy, I'd do it. After all, this was my weekend to have fun before being shipped off to Italy. I didn't need to drag it down with talk of my parents.

So I slipped my hand into his, and the pressure from his grip sent jolts of electricity up my arm. My hand looked tiny, enveloped in his. I pulled my gaze from our clasped hands and up to him. His lips were tipped up into a smile.

"Deal," I said as he slowly shook my hand.

I thought that he held onto my hand a tad longer than absolutely necessary, but I wasn't completely sure. My mind was having a hard time processing what was happening around me. It felt as if the world was moving at a slower pace than normal as I sat across from Jet.

I hoped it would keep feeling that way, especially since in just 48 hours I would be gone. If I could, I'd slow down time forever.

But, when he dropped his hand, effectively breaking our contact, I was pulled back to the normal passing of time. The Ferris wheel circled a few more times before it came to a stop and the attendant informed us it was time to get off.

Jet waited for me and smiled down at me as I passed by. We kept in step as we wandered around the pier.

We kept our conversations light. We talked about our favorite class in school and the sports we did—or did not—play. The sun made its way through the sky as Jet nodded toward the games he wanted to play.

It was nice, standing next to him, attempting to shoot baskets or blasting some creepy-looking plastic man with a water gun.

Even though I completely bombed every game I played, Jet actually won a few and let me pick the ridiculously expensive stuffed animal prize. I settled on a dolphin and tucked it under my arm as Jet nodded toward the exit. Then, realizing that I was going to be riding on a motorcycle, I gave the dolphin to a little boy with dyed-blue lips, who squealed and pumped it in the air.

Jet chuckled. "Ready for this portion of the day to be over?" he asked as he held out his hand.

I nodded. "Sure. What else did you have in mind?"

We moved through the building to the exit and back out onto the boardwalk.

Jet shrugged as he slipped his hands into his jacket pockets. "Dinner?"

My stomach rumbled. Apparently, fried dough covered with sugar wasn't very filling. "I'm starving."

Jet chuckled as he walked alongside me. "I know a place."

I nodded, keeping my gaze trained on the wood slats under my feet. "Oh really?"

But before Jet could answer, his phone rang.

He pulled it from his back pocket, and as he read the name on the screen, his face fell. After a quick glance over at me, he swiped to answer. "Hey, man," he said as he held the phone to his ear.

I kept silent as I walked next to him. I couldn't make out what the person was saying, but I could hear the tone—and it didn't sound good.

"You what?" Jet asked as he moved to one side of the pier. He pressed his finger into his other ear as he leaned on the railing. "What were you thinking?"

A more panicked voice sounded from the other end.

Jet's jaw clenched and his gaze hardened.

I wanted to say something. I wanted to help. But I figured trying to insert myself into his conversation was probably not the smartest thing to do, so I remained silent.

"Yeah, I'll come get you. Hold tight." He growled as he pressed the end call button. After slipping the phone into his back pocket, he brought up both his hands and pushed them through his hair, staring out at the ocean.

"Everything okay?" I asked. I gave him a small, *I come in peace* smile.

Jet flicked his gaze down at me and then sighed as he shook his head. "I've got to call it, Brielle."

I stared at him. What did that mean? He must have seen my confusion, because he scrubbed his face with his hands.

"It's been fun, but I've got to go. I've got a life I have to get back to." He leaned closer to me. "And so do you."

Tears pricked my eyes as I started to shake my head. "No. No. You promised me a weekend. I...paid you. I trusted you." I stared hard at the ground, willing myself to get control of my frustration. This wasn't what I wanted to do. I wanted to be strong no matter how weak I felt. But this was yet another part of my life that I had absolutely no say in.

"Brielle, please..." His shoes came into view as he moved closer. He reached out and rested his hand on my elbow, like that was going to somehow make me feel better.

It didn't.

If anything, it made me madder. "You made a promise," I said. "You told me I could trust you." My voice was low as I glanced up at him.

He studied me with his eyebrows furrowed. "Things have changed."

I shook my head, this time more resolutely. "Not good enough. Take me with you. I promise, I won't get in the way. I just...I can't go home right now."

He looked like he was fighting an internal battle. "Bri—"

"I promise. You won't even know I'm there."

He pressed his lips together, and then, after what felt like an eternity, he sighed. "Fine. But the minute there's trouble, I want you gone. You'll call your family and work out whatever drama is going on between you."

I held up my left hand. "I swear."

His eyes narrowed as he glanced over to my hand. He turned to make his way down the boardwalk, and I followed. But as soon as he'd started, he stopped. Before I could catch myself, I plowed into him. Startled, I looked up to see what was wrong.

Being the graceful person that I was, I stumbled, my body pitching forward. Luckily, Jet seemed more aware of his surroundings than I. His hands wrapped around my waist to steady me. Heat flushed my body as I glanced up at him. He was staring down at me with an intensity that I couldn't quite read.

What was he thinking?

Then his intensity turned to confidence. "You okay?" he asked.

Embarrassment coursed through me, but I found enough control to slowly nod. "Yes."

He held my gaze and then a smooth smile spread across his lips. Like he wanted to make sure I understood what he was about to say. "I call the shots. When I say it's time for you to go home, you go home," he said.

It took a moment for his words to catch up with my brain. He was in charge and could tell me to go home whenever he wanted. I wasn't sure how I felt about that.

"But—"

He shook his head, halting my protest. "It's that or nothing."

I chewed my cheek before I blew out a breath and nodded. "I understand."

He dropped his hands as he studied me a moment longer. "Come on. Let's get out of here."

CHAPTER SIX

A sense of freedom washed over me as I sat on the back of Jet's motorcycle. It was like I was a bird let out of its cage for the first time. With my arms wrapped around Jet and the expansiveness of the world around me, I felt untouchable. There were no rules. No parents to squash me into submission.

I was just...me.

Adrenaline pumped through my veins as I tightened my grip on Jet's waist. We leaned together as he took the corner and headed to the outskirts of Atlantic City. A place where my parents would never be caught dead.

It was perfect.

I was enjoying this little escapade. For the first time in a long time, I was making my own decisions. And I loved it. I couldn't imagine going back to my stuffy life as Brielle Livingstone, heiress to the Livingstone Hotel empire.

There was so much responsibility wrapped up in that

name, and most times, it felt like a noose around my neck. Like a part of myself that I was never going to get away from. But here, on the back of Jet's motorcycle, it didn't matter.

It didn't take long before Jet pulled into the parking lot of Tommy's Convenience Store and turned off the engine. My ears rang as silence settled around us. I waited for Jet to kick the stand down before I climbed off.

My legs felt wobbly, and I could still feel the rumble of the motorcycle throughout my body. I reached up to unbuckle my helmet and slip it off. Then I placed it on the back of Jet's bike and straightened.

Jet climbed off the motorcycle and tucked the key into his front pocket.

I turned to study the store behind us. "Thirsty?" I asked, nodding in the direction of the very large slushy cup in the window.

Jet shook his head. "We're here to help someone."

"Who?"

He glanced down at me as he passed by. "Just keep quiet," he said.

I pinched my lips together as I nodded and followed him. He held the door open as I walked into the small store. Displays were lined along the walls. They were stocked with all sorts of candy and chips.

The far back wall had coolers filled with bottles and cans. A soda fountain was tucked into the corner next to a slushy machine with an Out-of-Order sign taped to the front.

Well, that was disappointing.

"I warned you boys." A tall man with thinning hair moved into my line of sight. He'd stepped out from behind the counter, and I could see his stained shirt and yellowing teeth.

He had the look of death on his face. Out of instinct, I stepped closer to Jet—he didn't seem phased by this man.

"I know, Mr. McCabe. I don't know what came over Crew. I'll take care of him."

Mr. McCabe folded his arms, and I could see the faded mermaid tattoo across his forearm. I wondered for a moment if it was one of the tattoos that wiggled when he moved his muscles.

"It'll cost you," he said.

I peeked over at Jet, suddenly feeling like I was in a mafia movie. What did Crew do, and what was Jet going to have to do to repay Mr. McCabe? I kept my lips shut but silently willed someone to help clue me in.

Jet's lips were drawn into a tight line and his jaw muscles twitched. He narrowed his eyes at Mr. McCabe. "How much?"

A sick smile spread across Mr. McCabe's lips. Sort of like a hunter who discovers he has something caught in his trap. "Two hundred."

Jet scoffed as he shook his head. "I ain't got that kind of money, and you know it."

Mr. McCabe shrugged. "Not my problem, boy. Your friend should learn to control his fingers." He leaned in. "Before he finds himself without any."

A shiver rushed down my spine as I glanced up at Jet. Thankfully, Jet looked a lot calmer than I felt. I was completely unprepared for this rescue? Shakedown? I wasn't sure what was happening.

"You talk a big game, but we both know the reason you can't and won't call the cops. So let's settle this like gentlemen instead of swindlers." Jet reached into his back pocket and pulled out the wad of twenties I'd given him.

Somehow—I wasn't sure how—he made it look like there were very few bills in that pile as he handed five of them over.

"I need the last one to get my kid sister some dinner, but you can have what's left." He motioned toward the bills.

Mr. McCabe studied Jet's hand. "Give me the last twenty and you'll have yourself a deal."

Jet hesitated, and then, through slight-of-hand, slipped the last bill out of the pile as he handed it over—keeping the rest of the stack hidden. "You're a crook, you know that?"

Mr. McCabe greedily grabbed the money and shoved it into his pocket. "And you need to find better friends. They keep costing you money."

Jet slipped his hand—and the rest of the twenties—into his back pocket. Then he shrugged. "Forgive me if I don't take life advice from someone with your background." He nodded toward the back. "We had a deal. Now let Crew go."

Mr. McCabe turned and spat tobacco into the trash and then shrugged. "Dumb kids," he said as he reached into his pocket and pulled out a jumble of keys. After finding the right one, he slipped the key into the lock and turned it, exposing a small room filled to the brim with filing cabinets and a solid wood desk that took up entirely too much space.

As he pushed open the door further, a baseball cap came into view. Crew—or that's who I assumed it was—tipped his head up and smiled at Jet. "You came."

Jet didn't respond as he stared at Crew. Then he waved toward the door. "Let's go."

Crew stood and sauntered out of the room. He winked at Mr. McCabe as he tapped him on his shoulder. "See you later," he said as he walked past us and out the door.

Jet was staring off into the distance. He looked as if he were carrying the world on his shoulders. I wanted to say something, anything, to help him feel better, but everything I thought of sounded lame.

Truth was that any sort of support I could give him felt hollow. I didn't know what he was going through. I'd never had a friend who needed me to pay his way out of trouble.

Jet turned, glanced down at me for a moment, and then made his way to the door. "Let's go," he said.

I smiled briefly at Mr. McCabe and followed Jet out of the store.

As we stepped outside, Mr. McCabe called out, "Nice doing business with you," before his sadistic laughter filled the air. The door slowly closed behind us, muffling the sound as it shut.

Now free from that dingy place, I took in a deep breath and glanced around. Crew was standing at the far end of the parking lot. He would occasionally reach down and grab a rock, straightening up to throw it into the small patch of woods next to the store.

Jet stormed over. Not sure what to do, I followed but kept my distance.

"What the hell was that?" Jet asked when he reached Crew. He pushed Crew's shoulder, making him stumble.

Crew cursed under his breath and turned. Even from where I was standing, I could see the fire in Crew's eyes. He parted his lips as if he was going to let Jet have it, but then he clenched his jaw and shook his head.

"That was money my family needed," Jet said. "Why did you do that? Again?" Jet ran his hands through his hair as he began to pace. He kept his arms up, his elbows pointed toward the sky as he entwined his hands behind his head.

Crew chucked a handful of rocks into the bushes and sighed. "I'm sorry, man. I just..." His gaze flicked over to me and then back to Jet. "Who's the girl?"

Jet's gaze snapped over to me. He looked startled, as if he hadn't expected me to be standing there. Then he glanced back at Crew. "Leave her out of this. She's a friend."

Crew scoffed as his gaze roamed over me. "Since when does a *friend* of yours wear pearls?" His gaze lingered at my neck, and out of instinct, my hand moved to cover my necklace.

Jet slapped Crew's face. "Hey. Eyes over here. Ignore her. I want you to tell me how you're going to pay me back."

Crew growled as he whipped his gaze over to Jet. They stood there, in this strange, challenging stance. As if they were sizing each other up.

Thankfully, Jet was a few inches taller and wider than Crew. After a few minutes of this head-to-head stare down, Crew sighed and his shoulders relaxed. "I'll pay you back."

Jet nodded. "I've heard that before. Do you have an idea as to how you're going to do that? Last I checked, you were broke."

Crew glanced over at me for a moment and then leaned toward Jet. "Not when a girl who looks like she belongs in a rich teenage sitcom is standing right there. Last thing I need is for her to be spilling my secrets to her daddy."

I glanced down at my clothes. I thought they were normal, but now I was starting to doubt my fashion sense. Did I dress rich?

Jet shook his head. "You can't start that again. We'll find another way." He reached out and rested his hand on Crew's shoulder. It seemed as if his frustration for his friend had died down and all that was left was a strange sense of understanding.

I watched them, wondering what their story was. Wondering if Jet would ever tell me.

Crew raised the same arm and held onto Jet's shoulder. "I've got your back like you've got mine. I'll fix this."

They stood in silence for a moment before Jet nodded. "I know."

An uncomfortable feeling grew in my stomach as I watched them. It was like I was intruding. I swallowed as I dropped my gaze. I felt like an idiot. I didn't belong there.

My stomach twisted with an ache I knew all too well. I didn't belong there. I didn't belong anywhere. Maybe I was a fool to push myself on Jet like this. After all, when everything was said and done, where was I going to end up?

Right back where I started.

Jet and Crew stepped back, and, after a bro-shake, Crew promised to call and then took off down the road. It didn't take long before he disappeared down a side street, leaving me and Jet alone.

So many questions plagued my mind as I watched Jet study the ground, pushing a rock around with his shoe. He was lost in thought, and I almost didn't want to disturb him.

But I didn't want to stand there and stare at him any longer, so I walked over and stopped next to him. He didn't acknowledge me. I softly cleared my throat and peered over at him.

"Everything okay?" I asked.

Jet glanced at me as he let his breath out slowly. Then he shoved his hands into his jacket and shrugged. "This is my life. If you can't handle it, you can always go home." He turned and made his way over to his bike.

My feet felt rooted to the pavement as his words washed over me. What did that mean? Why would he assume that I couldn't handle it?

Sure, Mr. McCabe was a little unnerving, but I hadn't freaked out. I was used to strange, older men. In my experience, to be a billionaire you had to be somewhat of a social outcast. And the fact that Jet thought I was going to crumble at the first sign of struggle made me mad.

I wasn't weak.

Frustration raced across my skin and heated my whole

body. I wasn't going to stand by and let someone dictate what I could or couldn't handle. He didn't know me, and it was laughable that he thought he did.

"Excuse me," I said as I stood in front of his bike so he would have to look at me.

He reached out and rested his hands on the handles of the bike. He glanced up at me with an exasperated look. It only made me angrier.

"You don't know me," I said, leaning in as my voice lowered.

He quirked an eyebrow. "What?"

I waved at him. "This? Whatever this is? Don't think for a second, I can't handle whatever *your world* throws at me."

A soft smile twitched his lips as he leaned back and folded his arms. "My world?"

The fact that he was entertained by my frustration just made me more upset. "This gangster, Godfather world you live in." I pointed at him. "Don't treat me like I'll break. I won't."

His gaze trailed over to my finger and then back up to meet my gaze.

"Godfather?"

I threw my hands up in the air. "Is this how you fight? Repeat whatever the other person says?"

"We're fighting?"

I growled as I shot him my best death stare and folded my arms. I stalked over to the side of the parking lot where the grass grew uninhibited. I really didn't want to look at Jet right now.

If I was honest with myself, my little fit had nothing to do with him. I was just tired of being told what I could or couldn't handle. My parents spent most of my life treating me like I would break. That I would make the wrong decisions if given the chance. That it would somehow reflect badly on them in the end.

They decided everything for me. And I never had a say.

For the first time in my life, I was choosing something for myself, but now Jet was taking that away from me. I needed freedom, and it wasn't until I got a taste of it that I realized how much I'd been craving it.

All the frustration and disappointment that I'd felt over the years settled in my throat. I swallowed, hoping to dislodge it. I couldn't break down. Not now. Jet would definitely think he'd saddled himself with a crazy girl and drive me right back to the hotel. My moment of peace would be over before it started.

The crunching of gravel sounded behind me, and I shivered at the thought of Jet coming for me. It excited and scared me at the same time. Then I remembered the wad of cash stuck in my bra, and I realized what he was really coming for.

I was his payday. He wasn't going to drop me off anywhere until he was guaranteed his money.

Great.

I cursed the butterflies that were racing around in my stomach. They were annoying and definitely didn't belong there. I was losing my focus and I couldn't have that happen.

"You okay?" Jet's soft voice settled around me. I glanced

over to see him standing next to me, his shoulders inches from mine.

I pinched my lips together and nodded. "Yeah," I whispered.

He peeked down at me. He had a slightly amused, but mostly genuine look in his eyes. Like he was asking me to forgive him without actually saying it.

"My world...it's complicated."

I turned and parted my lips, but he must have anticipated my pushback, because his hands were up as if to stop me.

"And I'm sure yours is complicated as well."

At least he'd picked up on that. I nodded as I pinched my lips together. I was interested in what he had to say and felt somewhat confident that what I'd said was sinking in.

"But my kind of complicated"—he sighed—"I can't get you mixed up in it."

I could understand that even if I didn't want to. I was being selfish as well. I was mixing him up with my kind of complicated. I'm sure Dad wasn't going to take the news that I'd left lightly. And the person caught with me...well, that was a gamble I was making him take without him really knowing he was taking it.

"I understand," I said as I studied the ground. How had my life come to this? This wasn't the way I'd seen my future going. I feared the passing of time. Every minute that ticked by was a minute closer to me leaving.

And as much as I wanted to stop the forward movement of the present, I couldn't. Time was going to pass if I was standing here in the parking lot with Jet or in my hotel room with Stefano. Right now, I just wanted to be in charge of that time. If only for a few more hours.

I deserved this.

So I turned and gave him the biggest smile I could muster. "I'm fine. I'll be fine," I said as I dipped down to meet his gaze.

He glanced up. "I know."

"Besides, it's only for a short time. I'm sure you can handle me for a little while longer. Then I'll be out of your hair."

He squinted an eye as he studied me. "Is that a promise?"

I held up my left hand and nodded. What I really wanted to say was that it was a guarantee, but that was a thread I didn't want to pull at. He didn't need to know I was leaving in a few days. And I didn't want to be reminded.

This weekend was about forgetting my life. Living it the way I wanted to live it.

And I was going to make sure that nothing stood in the way of that.

Jet studied me for a moment before he laughed and nodded toward his bike. "Come on, let me take you somewhere."

I quirked an eyebrow. "Where?"

He shrugged as he walked backwards toward his bike. "You'll just have to trust me." But then he held up his left hand in a teasing way. "But I promise it will be less...what did you say? Godfather-y?"

I shook my head as a laugh escaped my lips. Jet seemed

to take that as agreement because he turned and threw his keys into the air in a smooth, swift movement.

Just as I took a step toward him, my phone vibrated. I turned and slipped it out of my bra. My heart stuttered to a stop when I saw the name sprawled across the screen.

Mom.

CHAPTER SEVEN

I don't know why I hadn't thought of the fact that Mom could simply call me during my ridiculous runaway plot. I guess I had been too busy enjoying myself and trying to forget the world I was running away from.

I had no room in my head for thoughts of Mom and Dad.

But here I was, staring down at my phone in the middle of a parking lot in a part of town that would make Mom would faint if she heard I was here.

It buzzed in my hand. The vibration slowly pushed its way into my head, forcing me to acknowledge the fact that my parents were on the other end.

Right. Mom was just going to keep calling until I answered. And her worry and suspicion would only increase each time she called.

I pressed the button and brought the phone to my ear. "Hello?"

"Well, I hope you're finished with your tantrum and are ready to come back up."

I stared at the trees in front of me, shifting in the breeze. Did she seriously think that I was still standing downstairs? Wow.

"No, I'm not," I said with the calmest voice I could muster.

She scoffed. "Are you here? In the suite?"

I heard some shifting. I could imagine exactly where she was. Sprawled out on her cream couch with her legs up. Not bothered enough to stand to see if her daughter was in the house.

"No, Mom. I'm not home. And I'm not coming back until Monday."

"Brielle!" she yelled, followed by a bunch of sputtering.

"What's wrong?" Dad's booming voice sounded through the receiver.

"Brielle is running away."

"What? Is she a child?"

I sighed. I hated when they talked like I wasn't there. I was always a second thought, even during their fights.

"Young lady, enough is enough. We promised the Espositos that we would go to dinner with them, and you will be there."

I pinched my lips together and shook my head. I felt a bit stupid, but the movement helped me feel in control. "No. No, I'm not. I'll be back after the weekend. I'm going to spend some time on my own before I start my meticulously planned life."

"Planned? This is for your future. It's your duty."

I swallowed. My parents hadn't always been like this. It must be the stress of running a huge hotel that had turned them into these monsters. But as much as I wanted to excuse my parents' terrible behavior, I couldn't. They weren't the loving people I remembered, and right now, I wanted nothing to do with the life that they felt was *so* important.

I wanted freedom and I was going to take it.

"Fine. Then it will be my duty on Monday. For now, I'm going to be me. I'm going to live." I took in a deep, shaky breath. I wish I sounded stronger. Perhaps I was in denial. But right now, denial sounded pretty dang good.

Mom was sputtering again on the other end of the phone. She was muffled by Dad's deep sighs.

I waited, hoping to see if I could appeal to the softer side of the Livingstones.

"I'll be safe and sound at home by Sunday night. I promise." I'd been nothing but an amazing daughter to my parents since I was old enough to have an opinion. They had no reason to distrust me.

The phone fell silent and I could practically hear the wheels turning in Dad's mind. From his hesitation, I could sense that he was weighing the pros and cons. Definitely the businessman in him.

He was trying to figure out if the work it would take to fight me on this was worth it.

"You promise?" he asked. His voice had grown softer.

His telltale sign that he was about to give in. Good. This was where I wanted him.

"Cross my heart."

"Fine. Back home Sunday night." He paused. "Who are you with anyway?"

I glanced over at Jet, who'd settled back on his motorcycle and was fiddling with his phone. There was absolutely no way I could tell him about Jet. Dad would swallow his tongue and still find a way to demand that I return home.

"Kate."

Note to self, call her and tell her she's my scapegoat.

I hated lying, especially when I dragged my friend into it. But I needed this, even if it wasn't rational.

"Fine. We'll see you on Sunday."

A slow smile spread across my lips as I fought the urge to pump my fists in the air. I had actually won—which in the Livingstone world was a rarity. I never won.

"Be safe."

"I will."

Dad mumbled something that sounded like "love you," but before I could confirm, the call ended.

I stared down at my phone as I took a deep breath. Well, at least that had ended in my favor. I didn't have to worry about my parents calling the cops on me and my weekend ending very differently than I expected.

I now had my freedom for twenty-four hours, and I was going to bask in every single second. This all I had left of my life before Mom and Dad took it over, and I was going to live it.

I slipped my phone into my back pocket and made my way over to Jet. He glanced over at me.

"Everything okay?" he asked.

I nodded as I reached out and grabbed the motorcycle helmet that was resting on the back seat. "Yeah. Just my parents wondering where I am."

I tried not to notice the look of relief that flashed across his face. "Everything okay? Do they want you home?"

I glared at him as I slipped the helmet on and buckled it. "Sorry. They gave me permission to stay out as long as I want, so..." I sucked in my breath and shrugged. "Looks like you're stuck with me."

Call me crazy, but I didn't want to see the look on his face as my statement settled around him. I held onto his shoulders as I swung my foot over the motorcycle. Once I was settled, I wrapped my arms around his waist.

The first thing I felt was the soft rattle in his chest as he laughed. Heat pricked my skin as he peered at me from over his shoulder.

"Why are you laughing?" I asked.

He shrugged as he started up the engine. "It's just strange. Someone thinking my life is a vacation when they come from what you do."

I pulled back. Jet didn't know what he was talking about. Sure, from the outside, my world looked amazing. When you had money, you had everything, right?

Wrong.

There was so much responsibility wrapped up in keeping the wealth, and people had a tendency to forget that money was hard to keep. Some people spent their entire lives as slaves to the dollars in their accounts.

And that was exactly what I was. A slave to the Livingstone name. There was no vacation there. I had responsibilities. "Duties" as Dad called them. And no matter how far I ran, I was never going to be able to shake them.

Right now, Jet's life felt free, and I was desperate for that freedom.

"We live different lives," I said as I leaned against him.

He hesitated. "We sure do."

I didn't have time to respond. He revved the engine and took off out of the parking lot. I held onto him as he sped down the road. The feeling of the salty air on my face made me close my eyes and take in a deep breath.

Even though Jet couldn't believe that I would consider his life free, I did. In my world, there weren't any motorcycles. No sun shining down on your skin, warming your soul. There was no hitting the road and going anywhere you wanted.

For now, his life was my escape, and I was going to enjoy it.

Ten minutes later, he pulled into the driveway of a small, white two-story house. The paint was dingy and chipping. The grass out front needed to be cut—it hit me about midcalf when I climbed off his motorcycle.

Toys littered the yard, and bikes leaned against two trucks that looked as if they hadn't budged in a decade. The garage door wasn't closed all the way. There was about a foot between the bottom of the door and the ground.

I unbuckled my helmet and glanced over at him.

His skin looked flushed, and I wasn't sure if it was because of embarrassment or the late-afternoon sun.

He pushed the kickstand down and rested his motorcycle on it. Then he swung his leg off and straightened. I set the helmet down on the back.

"Home sweet home," he said as he stared at his house.

I nodded. "It's nice."

He scoffed. "Yeah. Sure. It's a piece of crap. I mean, it's no Livingstone Hotel."

"So, it looks lived in." That was more than I could say about the penthouse suite Mom and Dad occupied. It never looked like a home, with random knickknacks everywhere. Instead, it was just as sterile as one of the guest suites. Tacky hotel art adorned the walls. There were no family pictures or any indication that a family lived there. It was as lonely as my life felt.

"Well, if that's the measure we use to gauge the niceness of a house, then yes, ours is definitely lived in." He nodded toward the side door and I followed after him.

Just as he reached to grab the handle, the door swung open, and a very frantic woman appeared. Her dark hair matched Jet's, save the threads of grey that weaved through the pile on top of her head.

She had readers that hung from her neck and rested on top of the familiar light-blue uniform of the Livingstone Hotel's maid staff.

Her forehead wrinkled as her tired eyes scanned me and then Jet.

"Where have you been? I'm going to be late."

Jet shoved his hands through his hair as he shrugged. "Sorry. I had to help Crew get out of trouble."

His mom waved her hand at him with annoyance. "What did I tell you about hanging around the Jones kid? He's nothing but trouble, and that's the last thing you need." She held his gaze, and, from the intensity that passed over both of their countenances, I could tell she was hinting at a much deeper issue.

Curiosity bubbled up inside of me, but I just pushed it down. Jet had things about his life he was hiding—so did I. What did it matter if I didn't know what his were? I had no intention of telling him mine.

He was my freedom sensei right now. That was all.

My ridiculously good-looking freedom sensei, but I was going to push that little tidbit from my mind right now. No need to conflate the two things.

"Ma—" Jet started, but his mom just held up her hand.

"I don't have the energy right now. I'm late, and I can't be late again." She nodded toward the house. "Cassidy is inside. She's watching some ridiculous reality show. Brit will be home later, so stay with Cassidy until Brit's shift ends." She narrowed her gaze as she leaned in. Like she was threatening Jet.

Jet didn't seem phased. just nodded. "I got it. I'm not going to go anywhere. I know my job."

His mom's gaze passed over me before returning to Jet. "And no shenanigans in my house." Her voice dropped.

My whole body flushed as I realized the implication of

what she was saying. She thought...Jet and me? I shook my head. "Oh, you don't have to worry about that. We're"—I waved between us—"just friends."

His mom's lips tipped up into a smile, but I could tell she wasn't really smiling. "Right. Well, with Jet, you never know, and I'd like to keep his little sister innocent as long as I can."

My lips parted but no words came. I'd never had a guy's family not like me. This was strange. Being stared at like I was about destroy the innocence of Jet's sister was strange.

"Mom. Please. You're going to be late." Jet nodded toward the white four-door sedan that was parked on the side of the road.

His mom nodded as she pushed her hand into her purse and pulled out her keys. "Feed Cassidy..." She took a deep breath, and a look of regret passed over her face. "And keep him away from her, okay?"

When I glanced over to Jet, I saw his jaw flex as he nodded. "Yep. Bye," he said.

I wondered who *he* was, but it didn't feel right to ask. Instead, I watched Jet's mom hurry down the driveway and climb into her car.

Jet had remained quiet as she sped off down the street and around the corner. I wasn't sure what I was supposed to say about what had happened between the two of them, so I just turned and gave Jet a small smile.

He was still staring off down the road, distracted with his thoughts. I almost wondered if he'd forgotten that I was standing there.

"Everything okay?" I asked as I moved closer to him.

Sure, we'd only just met, but I didn't like seeing him upset. Maybe it was because I knew what it was like to have less than favorable parents, and, from what I'd seen, that was a sentiment Jet was all too familiar with.

His gaze snapped over to me. He studied me for a moment before a wide smile passed over his face. It felt forced and disingenuous. Like it was something he'd practiced for a very long time.

"I'm great," he said as he climbed the few steps to the door and pulled it open. "Come on, I'll introduce you to Cassidy. She's the sane one in the family."

I nodded as I followed after him. He walked into a small kitchen, where he kicked off his shoes. He turned and nodded toward mine. "You can keep them on if you want. I'm not sure when the floor was cleaned last."

I shrugged as I slipped off my shoes. Mom had always insisted that I be polite, and keeping my shoes on went against that. Plus, I didn't mind. I was sure the house wasn't that dirty.

Jet walked through the galley kitchen and into the living room. Besides having the drapes pulled closed and boxes piled up along the far wall, it was a tidy house. A small girl with bright red hair was sitting on the couch with her legs crisscrossed, hugging a pillow. Her eyes were wide and her expression animated.

"Hey, Cass," Jet said as he walked through the room and plopped down next to her. She waved her hand in Jet's direction, telling him to shush.

"He's about to hand out the last rose," she whispered.

Not sure what to do, I walked over and sat on the other side of her. "The Bachelor?" I asked.

Cassidy nodded and turned to me. Just as her gaze met mine, she giggled. "Who are you?" she asked as she held out the remote and paused the TV.

"This is Brielle. She's paying me to show her around Atlantic City this weekend."

Cassidy giggled again as her gaze roamed over me. "Do you live here? Where did you get that dress? Your hair is so pretty," she said as she reached out to touch it.

I gave her a warm smile. Even though we'd just met, I liked her.

"Slow down, Question McGee. You've got to let her at least answer one." Jet poked Cassidy in the ribs, causing her to jerk and swat his hand away.

She climbed toward the back of the couch to get away from him. "Stop!" she squeaked as she wiggled away from him.

After scaling the back of the couch and then plopping safely on my other side, she glared at Jet and stuck her tongue out at him. He raised his hands before stretching out on his half of the couch.

"My plan worked," he said as he placed his hands behind his head and winked at me.

Cassidy didn't seem as charmed by his expression as I was. Instead, she shook her head.

"With you here, we'll get him back," she said, lifting her hand as she whispered in my ear.

"Really?" I asked under my breath.

Jet furrowed his brows. "What are you two doing? No plotting allowed in this house." He straightened as he stuck his finger in Cassidy's direction. "You can't get other people to fight your battles for you."

Cassidy's jaw dropped. "It's not fair that I can't recruit backup. I mean, I am nine years old. I should get a break."

Jet shrugged as he leaned forward to grab Cassidy's discarded pillow. He propped it up behind him. "Check the rule book."

I glanced between the two of them. "There's a rule book?"

Cassidy groaned as she stood and made her way over to the shelf to the left of the TV. She pulled out a worn notebook from a stack of books, then she returned to the couch and leaned into me.

"We started this two years ago, when Jet was put in charge of babysitting me," she said as she flipped the cover open. In it were pages of rules. No eye gouging. No hair pulling...the list went on and on.

"Wow," I said as I pointed to the *no fighting on the first or third Sunday* rule. "You guys are thorough."

Jet nodded. "When you're battling this one, you have to be."

Cassidy gasped. "What? You're the cheater."

Jet shook his head. "See, that's exactly what a cheater would say."

Cassidy scrunched up her face as she glared at Jet. "Ooo. You're so dead," she said. She sprang up from the couch, sprinted down the hall, and slammed her door.

I glanced back at Jet, who was chuckling to himself.

"What happens now?"

He wiggled his eyebrows as he leaned over the side of the couch and returned with a shield made of tinfoil.

"We battle."

CHAPTER EIGHT

I slipped behind a large bush in the backyard and crouched behind Cassidy who was peeking around the leaves. She giggled as she turned and made some movement with her hand around her face. I furrowed my brow as I attempted to decipher it.

"What?" I whispered as I leaned in closer to her.

She sighed—emphasis on the eye roll—and nodded for me to lean in. "He's hiding back here somewhere, I know it," she said as she pushed up her makeshift helmet with a hand that was clutching a foam sword made from a pool noodle and a dowel.

I peeked through the foliage to see a broken trailer, a tipping shed, and a few half-motorcycles scattered throughout the backyard. The long grass tickled my legs, and I found myself slapping it away like they were mosquitos.

"So what do we do?" I asked as she shoved one of her

foam swords into my hand.

"We need to get to the amulet before he does," she said, nodding toward the fence that lined the back of their yard. A small trophy could be seen in the middle of the sun-faded planks.

"That's what we are trying to get?" I asked, swatting at another offending bit of grass.

She nodded.

"And what do we win if we get it?"

A very serious expression passed over her face. "We don't have to cook dinner."

That was a mission I could get on board with.

"Perfect," I said as I crouched down and began scanning the yard.

"Now, you try to get the amulet while I come up the back. I'm smaller than you and can slink better." She crouched down onto the ground to show me.

"Got it," I said as I hunched over and pretended to tiptoe away from our hideout.

"Wait," she squeaked.

I hesitated after her hand gripped my arm.

"He's very cunning," she said. The intensity of her stare caused me to smile.

"I think I can handle it."

One of her eyes narrowed as she studied me. "That's what Brooke said."

I blinked a few times. "Brooke?"

She rolled her eyes, like she couldn't believe she was having to go over this. "His other girlfriend." She got a disgusted look on her face. "He brought her here, and she *said* she was going to get the amulet..." She sighed dramatically, her chest rising in a purposeful movement.

"And?" I asked as I leaned in, hoping she couldn't see the jealousy that was creeping up inside of me. I wasn't sure I wanted to hear what Jet and Brooke had been doing back here.

"And I found them kissing in the grass." She stuck her tongue out as she shook her head.

And there it was. The exact thing I didn't want to hear.

Jet kissing anyone made me feel sick. And then my thoughts returned to Jet kissing me.

Heat rushed across my skin as the feeling of Jet's lips on mine came crashing into my mind. I swallowed, my mouth drying up as I studied her. I don't know why I was reacting this way. I mean, just because he did that with some girl named Brooke, didn't mean he was going to do that with me.

"Brielle?" she asked, leaning in.

"Yeah, mm-hm?" The heat of the evening air mixed with my thoughts and settled on my cheeks. What was the matter with me?

"Are you ready?" she asked as she held up her pinkie finger.

I nodded as I curled my own pinkie around hers. "Get the amulet," I said.

"And don't kiss Jet."

"Yes." Thankfully, she took off after our promise, so I didn't have to say anything more. I watched as she sprinted through the grass and dove behind one of the discarded garbage cans.

With her gone, I focused my thoughts on the small trophy in front of me.

I could do this. How hard could it be?

Plus, I wanted to win. One, because I didn't want to cook dinner, and, two, because I liked Cassidy. She was sweet and untainted from the world. And, it was sort of heart-melting to see Jet interact with her. They had a bond that I would never have, being an only child.

I crouched down as I hurried past the crooked shed, and then I pushed my body up against the wall as I peeked around the corner.

Nothing.

Part of me wondered if Jet had snuck off, leaving me to hang out with his little sister. After all, I was just an annoying tagalong to him. Frustration pricked my skin, but I pushed it down. There was no need to get upset. And if he had, so what? I mean, Cassidy was fun to hang out with, and being here was ten times better than being with Stefano.

Which was what I would be doing had I stayed home.

After a few minutes of nothing, I gathered my courage and took a step toward the fence that was about ten feet away from me. If I rushed, I could grab the amulet and win.

But, just as my foot settled in the grass, I felt something jab me in the back.

"Hold it right there." Jet's low voice caused shivers to rush across my skin. He must be only inches from me because I could feel his body warmth cascade over me. "No sudden movements, or I'll impale you with my sword."

I peeked around to see he held an identical foam sword in his hand. His other hand wrapped around my arm and pulled it close to his chest.

"How did you know I was here?" I asked in my best damsel-in-distress voice.

His chuckle was soft and genuine. "Wow. Really hamming it up, aren't you?"

I shrugged as embarrassment settled on my cheeks. "Hey, when I go all in—I go all in."

"Duly noted," he said, his voice dropping down to a whisper.

"What's with the trophy?" I asked as my body began to relax. It was strange being this close to Jet. But also comforting.

He was just a stranger to me earlier this morning, but now? I don't know. It felt odd to say I was getting to know him—that we were becoming friends—but we kind of were. And I liked it.

"It was a trophy I won in the fourth grade," he said. His voice sent shivers down my back as he leaned in closer.

"For what?"

He was quiet for a moment. I peeked behind me to see that his face had stilled. If I didn't know better, I would have said he was blushing.

"Not going to tell you that," he said.

I dropped my jaw. "What?" Then I glanced back at the trophy. "Well, maybe I just need to get over there and see for myself." I turned to face him, trying to break his hold on me, but he must have anticipated my movement. His grip tightened on my arm, and suddenly, I was crashing into his chest.

"Oh, no you don't," he said, wrapping his arm around my waist. I was pinned to his very broad chest, and I couldn't help but feel the familiar muscles under his t-shirt. It was strange to be this intimately aware of his body.

My heart did a little pitter-patter as I peeked up at him.

There was a playful hint to his smile as he peered down at me. Like maybe he was enjoying our closeness as well.

I narrowed my eyes, hoping to mask the feelings that were bubbling up inside of me. I steadied my gaze as I met his. "What could you possibly want to hide from me..." I widened my eyes as I dropped my jaw. "Was it a Mr. America Pageant?"

He quirked an eyebrow. "Wow. Never in my life has anyone even hinted that I could participate in something like that." He leaned closer so we were inches apart. "Should I take that as a compliment?" he asked. I noticed a drop in his voice, and his words came out deep and breathy.

I swallowed. Emotions were running like runaway trains throughout my body. I wanted to melt into a puddle from the way he was looking at me and from the way it felt to have his body pressed against mine.

Like we were two puzzle pieces that fit perfectly together.

Which was ridiculous.

Jet was my distraction from my real life. He and I could

never be more than a weekend fling. After Sunday, my life was set.

Why was I allowing myself to think anything else could happen?

It wasn't fair to me, and it wasn't fair to him.

But I couldn't help the teasing smile that emerged on my lips. Sure, I couldn't date him, but I could flirt with him.

"I'm not telling," I said as I batted my eyelashes at him.

He chuckled, and I could feel the vibration through his chest. I involuntarily stretched my fingers out against his chest. His gaze flicked down to my hands and then back up to me. His eyebrows were furrowed as he studied me.

Suddenly, we weren't laughing. Instead, there was this tension that settled around us as he held my gaze.

The desire to flee took over me. My eyes widened as I attempted to straighten up, pushing against him as I planted my feet underneath me.

"Brielle, I..." he started, but his voice trailed off as he dropped his arms and stepped back. "Sorry," he said as he pushed his hands through his hair and glanced over at me. "I get a little competitive."

I giggled, hoping it would come out relaxed. It didn't. I sounded like a crazed clown. Perfect.

Heat flooded my skin, but I forced myself to shrug. "I get it. I'm competitive too."

Jet was studying me, and I couldn't help but fidget. Something between us had changed. There was an intensity to his look that made me wonder what he was thinking.

Was he thinking about me? Did I want to know?

But when I glanced up to look at Jet again, he was no longer focused on me. Instead, his jaw had dropped, and he was staring at something behind me.

He lunged forward, lifting his sword.

I blinked a few times as he raced by me. He yelled, "NO!" and reached out to grab Cassidy, who was climbing down the fence with the trophy in hand.

He pulled her off the fence and spun her around. She giggled this high-pitched laugh as she held the trophy high in the air.

"I won! I won!" she squealed, pumping her fists in the air.

Jet set her on the ground and then crouched down so he could look her in the eyes. "Darn you," he said as he reached up and tousled her hair. She protested, but the smile on her face remained as she wagged her finger at him.

"Our plan worked," she said, glancing at me and flashing her wide, missing-teeth smile.

I nodded as I brushed off my clothes. "Yep. We make a great team."

She hugged the trophy like it was the best thing in the world and nodded. Then she turned to face Jet. "Homemade chicken tenders, please," she said, batting her eyelashes.

Jet scoffed, but Cassidy didn't wait to hear his protest. She skipped back to the house, where I assumed she was going to watch her show again.

When I turned back to study Jet, my heart leapt into my throat. He was standing a foot away with his arms crossed and his eyes narrowed.

"So, that was just a game to you?" he asked, leaning in as if he wanted me to feel the full weight of his words.

"Yeah?" I asked, not sure what he was talking about.

He pushed his hand through his hair as he glanced over to where we'd been standing earlier. "And here I thought we were connecting." He got this shy look on his face, and I couldn't tell if he was being serious or not.

My mind flooded with a million thoughts, and I couldn't decide which one to listen to. I mean, there was no denying that I was attracted to Jet, but did that mean he felt the same about me?

And how did *I* feel about that?

Not good.

I wasn't sure if I should speak any of the words that were hanging on the tip of my tongue. They felt too raw. Too exposing.

He chuckled as he shook his head. "I'm just joking. Geez, you don't have to take everything so seriously," he said as he clapped his hand onto my shoulder. The force shook my whole body.

But that wasn't what I was focusing on. Anger crept up inside of me, and my hands found their way to my hips. I leaned in and narrowed my eyes. "You punk," I said, reaching out to shove his shoulder.

He held up his hands as he laughed. I swung again, and he dipped down and skittered to the side. "Hey, you played me. I had every right to return the favor."

I chased after him, but he knew his yard a lot better than I did. Just as I reached out to grab onto him, my foot got caught on a raised tree root, and suddenly I was falling to the ground.

Somehow, Jet turned at that exact moment, and I felt two arms wrap around me and change my trajectory. Instead of hitting hard dirt, I fell on top of Jet.

His breath left his lungs in a whoosh as he hit the ground. Stunned, I stared down at his closed eyes and the grimace on his face.

It felt like I was in shock. My whole body felt disassociated from me. I knew my hands were pressed against his chest. I knew his arms were wrapped around me. I knew my legs were tangled with his.

I knew all of this...but I was having a hard time processing it.

"I think you killed me," he said as he pinched his lips together.

"I'm so sorry," I whispered as I shifted to get off of him.

That just made his grip tighten more. "Wait," he said.

I stopped moving and just lay there. On top of Jet Miller. My shock wore off, and I was suddenly very aware of every part of my body touching every part of his.

Nerves settled in my stomach as I stared down at him. His eyes were still closed, but his face was more relaxed. I wondered what he was thinking. Was he as aware of our touching bodies as I was?

"Jet?" I asked. For my sanity, I needed to get up, to get some distance from him.

"Hmm?"

"Are you okay?"

He squinted up at me. The sunlight occasionally burst through the leaves of the tree above us. He studied me before releasing his grip.

"You okay?" he asked. I could feel him watching me as I pushed off of him and stood.

"Yeah, I think so," I said, brushing off my clothes.

He'd pulled himself up to sitting. His arm was draped on his knees and his other hand was behind him, holding his body weight. He looked a lot more relaxed than I felt. Maybe I was the only crazy person in the world that got all out of sorts when pressed against someone like Jet.

And that was just it. I *was* a crazy person. Why was I allowing these feelings to grow? Nothing could ever happen between us. Me being here was just a rebellious reaction to my parents. Jet and I could never be. There was no future to our story.

It ended Sunday night.

"Are you okay?" I asked again as I cleared my throat of all my ridiculous emotions and peered down at him.

He shrugged as he pushed off the ground and stood. Then he brushed off his pants. "I'll be fine," he said. He was only inches away from me. "I'm pretty tough."

My breath caught in my throat, and the only thing I could do was nod.

He smiled at me and then patted my shoulder. "Come on, it's time to make some fried chicken."

My jaw dropped as I followed after him. "Um, I believe you're the one who lost, not me."

He scoffed as he held open the back door. I stopped just before I went in so that I could stare him down.

He didn't seem to notice. "Well, you distracted me, and therefore, you help."

I shook my head. "That wasn't a rule."

"What do you know about the rules? Cassidy and I made them up. Therefore, I say you help cook."

I walked into the kitchen and could hear a woman squealing from the living room. Yep, Cassidy had gone back to her show.

"Cassidy?" I called, tipping my body toward the living room so I could be heard over the TV.

A second later, she appeared in the entryway between the kitchen and dining room.

"Do I have to help with dinner?" I asked.

She glanced at me and then behind me to Jet. She got a confused look before she shrugged. "I don't know. Ask Jet. He made up the rules." Then she disappeared.

Apparently, helping me was less interesting than watching her show.

Jet patted my head, and I reached up to push his hand away.

"See? Now, be a dear and grab the metal bowl from that cupboard," he said, nodding toward the cabinet behind me.

I glared at him as I made my way over to the sink and turned the water on. "I'll help, but under protest."

Jet joined me at the sink, sticking his hands in the water above mine. I growled as I reached over to flick soap bubbles in his direction.

He dodged out of the way and returned to the water stream. Thankfully, I'd finished washing my hands so I could step away from him.

My heart turned into a jackhammer every time he was around me. Putting distance between us made the most sense. I wandered over to the stove and grabbed a towel to dry my hands. I watched Jet as he finished washing up and shook the excess water from his fingers.

When he caught my eye, he smiled. He raised his hand and motioned toward the towel. I sighed as I threw it over to him.

Maybe I should ask him to drive me home. Maybe this was a complete mistake.

If how I was feeling kept growing, I was going to be in major trouble by the time the weekend was over. My life was on a path that I couldn't change. There was no reason to drag Jet into my mess.

But I'd be lying if I told myself that hanging out here was worse than being at the hotel. And maybe, just maybe, I wanted to see what would happen. Curiosity was really winning out. I wanted to know more about Jet.

I just had to be stronger. Be better at keeping my distance. I could do this. Feelings didn't have to get involved.

I let out my breath and walked over to the cupboard to grab a bowl. I set it on the counter and turned to him.

"I'm ready."

CHAPTER NINE

*J*et set out flour, milk, eggs, and chicken on the counter. He looked adorable in the apron he'd pulled out of a drawer. It was floral and matched the one he handed me.

I made a point to raise my eyebrows, which he shrugged off.

"Don't want those fancy clothes getting dirty," he said.

I just chuckled as I slipped the apron over my head and tied it in the back.

"Who knew you were so chivalrous," I said.

He smiled at me. "Oh, there's so much more to me that you don't know." He chuckled as he set a pot on the stove and began pouring oil into it.

I stood rooted to the spot. It felt more like a challenge than just something people said. Truth was, the more I was getting to know Jet, the more I realized there was more to him than met the eye.

104 | ANNE-MARIE MEYER

For starters, there was his adorable sister and how he acted around her. The fact that he'd taken pity on me—the crazy girl from behind the hotel. And how he'd helped his friend, despite having to give away his money.

There was a lot more to him, and I wanted to know everything there was to know about him.

Heat rushed to my cheeks, so I turned toward the ingredients he'd set out on the counter, determined to look busy.

"What can I do to help?" I asked, reaching out and fiddling with the milk jug.

"Ever make fried chicken?"

I shook my head. "I've never really cooked at all. We've always had a chef or just eaten at the restaurant." I glanced over to see him studying me.

There was a soft hint of a smile on his lips. When my gaze met his, he held it for a moment before grabbing a stack of bowls from the cupboard above me.

"Well, consider this your first cooking lesson," he said as he set the bowls out in front of me.

I rubbed my hands together. "Perfect."

He grabbed the flour and poured it into one of the bowls. "It goes milk, flour, egg, flour. Repeat. Oil," he said, pointing to each ingredient and then ending at the pot.

I nodded as he listed each item, but by the time he got to the end, I'd forgotten half of it. "Um..."

He chuckled. "I'll be here, don't worry. I won't let you go astray."

I chewed my lip as I peeked over at him. For some

reason, I wanted those words to mean more than they did. And I didn't realize how much I wanted them to mean more, until I heard them escape from his lips.

Of course, in my ridiculously vulnerable state, I was clinging to the one person who didn't seem to want to dictate how I lived my life. With Jet, I could just be me. I didn't have to worry about who I was supposed to be.

It meant a lot that he'd whisked me away right before my life crumbled down around me. I'd be grateful to him forever. Suddenly, the thousand dollars I'd agreed to pay him didn't seem like enough. He was doing so much for me, I wanted to return the favor.

"Thanks," slipped from my lips before I could stop it. I didn't want to get all sentimental on him, but, probably because I was slowly losing my mind, I wanted him to know that it meant a lot to me. What he was doing.

Jet stopped moving and turned to study me. I couldn't help but raise my gaze up to meet his. I wanted him to see how much I appreciated what he'd done for me.

"For what?"

I tucked my hair behind my ear and shrugged. "For agreeing to take me along on this crazy journey."

He paused as he held my gaze. "Sure. You are paying, though."

I nodded. "I know. But you didn't have to help me out. I appreciate it."

His expression softened, and my body felt light as he studied me. I could tell there was an internal battle going on inside of him. I wanted to reach out, to tell him that I hadn't meant for it to sound so clingy, but he stepped back before I could.

"Brielle," he said. His voice had dropped, and it sounded...worried.

I swallowed, wishing I could take it back. I didn't mean for it to come out like he was my knight in shining armor or anything. Or like we were going to be anything beyond this weekend. I just wanted him to know I was grateful.

"It's okay. Just forget I said anything." I forced a smile and then turned to the chicken. I stuck my finger through the plastic to puncture the seal. I needed to focus on something else while I forced down the feelings of rejection that had risen in my chest.

I was being ridiculous. I shouldn't be sad about this. We were a business transaction. That was it. I was the idiot who decided to read into things.

Jet appeared beside me, his arm brushing mine. I winced as I tried to pull away, but there was a wall on my other side, making retreat impossible.

"Listen, I..." He rested both hands on the counter in front of him as he dipped his head down. "I didn't mean that. I just...we live different lives. I would never fit in where you live." He glanced over at me, and I saw sadness in his gaze. "And you wouldn't fit in here."

I blinked—probably a bit too fast—and nodded. "Of course. Yeah. I understand." I motioned between the two of us. "Different worlds. I get it."

Ugh. From the tone of my voice and my frantic movements, I was doing a terrible job convincing him that I was
fine. I was a mess, and I was slowly revealing that mess
to Jet.

I was just giving him even more reason to drop me back
off at the hotel and leave. Which I wouldn't blame him for.
I'd return me too.

When I glanced back up to him, I saw that he was
watching me.

Embarrassment rushed through me, but I forced myself
to smile instead. "What's next?" I asked as I held up the
package of chicken tenders.

He furrowed his brows for a moment before he sighed
and stood. I could tell he still wanted to talk about this, but I
didn't. And I was grateful that he was willing to move on.

"Flour," he said, pulling the bowl closer to me.

We worked in unison until the smell of fried chicken
filled the air. My mouth watered as I watched Jet pull the
perfectly brown chicken strips from the oil and set them on
a paper towel.

Cassidy must have noticed as well because she wandered
into the kitchen and stood next to me.

"Wow," she said, leaning toward me.

"I know, right?"

She giggled. "Jet's the best cook. That's why I have to
beat him every time."

I smiled down at her. She was so sweet. Exactly what I'd
wanted in a little sister.

The more I thought about it, the more I envied Jet's life. Sure, his parents were stressed and probably not stellar, but he had an adorable sister and the freedom I craved.

Jet turned around and must have caught me smiling because he glanced down at Cassidy and then back up at me with his eyes narrowed. "I'm not sure I like the two of you talking."

Cassidy pressed her hand to her chest. "Me? Why?"

He held out his tongs and pointed them at her. "You're plotting something."

Cassidy shook her head and held up her hand like she was swearing in court. That must be where Jet got it from. "Promise."

Jet held his gaze on her before moving it to me. His tongs followed suit.

I laughed as I mimicked Cassidy. "I swear. We aren't plotting anything."

Jet hesitated before he laughed. "Well, even if you were, it wouldn't matter. No one is smarter than me. I would just thwart your plans."

Cassidy gasped as she dove for his knees. "What about this?" she asked as she yanked hard—trying to pull him down.

Jet laughed as he set the tongs down on the counter and pulled his sister off his legs. "Cassidy, come on. Seriously?"

He pulled her up and spun her around. Her giggles turned into full-out laughs as she tipped her head back. Once Jet finished, he set her down, and she took a few wobbly steps over to me, where she leaned against the counter. Jet returned to the chicken in the pot.

Cassidy leaned over. "I'm going to get him one of these days," she whispered.

I nodded. "I'm sure you will."

Jet turned to us, halting our conversation. He pointed to the fridge. "Grab your condiments and a plate. Dinner is served." The last sentence he said with a French accent as he gave a deep bow.

Cassidy cheered as she opened the fridge and pulled out some honey mustard sauce. "What do you want, Bri?" she asked, glancing over at me.

I smiled as I peered into the fridge. "Do you have ranch?"

She nodded as she pulled a bottle from the door. "Yep."

She handed it over and then proceeded to squeeze some mustard on her plate. Then, after grabbing a napkin, she made her way back into the living room, leaving Jet and I alone.

I tried to busy myself with the ranch bottle. I wasn't sure what to say to Jet, so I appreciated the distraction that getting my food ready gave me.

Jet was standing by me as I squeezed the ranch onto my plate. I couldn't help but notice how close he was. Or the fact that he was staring at me. I wanted him to move. I wanted him to stop watching me.

"Yes?" I asked when I finally couldn't take it anymore. I turned to stare at him, hoping he'd realize that I noticed him watching me.

He quirked an eyebrow, like he hadn't anticipated my

reaction. Then his gaze dipped down to the bottle in my hand. "Just waiting for the ranch."

I blushed as I glanced down at the death grip I had on the bottle. What was I thinking? That he was waiting for me?

Geez, I was an idiot.

I handed the bottle over, grabbed my plate and headed through the kitchen over to the living room.

"Hey, Brielle?"

Jet's soft voice washed over me, causing me to pause. I turned to see him studying me. There was this caring crease on his forehead that sent my heartbeat galloping. "Yeah?"

"Are we okay?"

I swallowed. I wasn't sure what we were. I was the idiot who was reading way too much into everything. I was the emotional basket case who was just trying to figure out her life. But I doubted that Jet was asking about that.

So instead of breaking down, I just nodded. "Of course. Why wouldn't we be?"

He hesitated before he smiled and shrugged. "You're right. Of course." He turned and grabbed his plate and started toward me.

Not wanting to be stuck walking next to him, I hurried into the living room and plopped down on one side of the couch. Cassidy was leaning over the other arm and using the side table to set her food on.

I placed my plate on my lap and picked up a chicken tender just as Jet came into view. He glanced over to

Cassidy and then to me. Like he wasn't sure where he was going to sit.

Then he shook his head and sat in the middle of us.

He weighed more than me, and I tipped toward him. After adjusting myself a few times, I was able to move close enough to the arm of the couch so that we wouldn't touch.

If Jet noticed, he didn't say anything. Instead, he leaned over to Cassidy.

"Can we please watch something else?" he asked. From the disdain in his voice, I could tell that reality TV shows weren't his cup of tea.

"But, Jet," Cassidy said in a whiny voice.

Jet stuck a finger in his ear. "Ugh, Cass. Not so loud."

She shrugged as she began eating again.

"Please?" he asked, pressing his hands together in front of him.

Cassidy sighed and held up the remote to change the station to the news. A newscaster was on the screen, talking about a huge announcement.

When they flashed to my dad's face, I yelped. What was he doing on the news?

"Turn it up," I said, waving my hand toward her.

Cassidy complied.

"...We're excited to announce the construction of two more Livingstone Hotels," Dad said. The camera panned to the empty lot he was standing in front of.

"Livingstone Inc. is partnering with Esposito International to fund the new luxury hotels."

Mr. Esposito filled the screen. Dad wrapped his arm

around Mr. Esposito's shoulders, which only made the man stiffen more.

"We are excited to bring our luxury hotels to Atlantic City," Mr. Esposito said in his thick accent.

Dad grinned as he reached out and shook hands with Mr. Esposito.

A rock felt like it had settled in my stomach. This was why Dad wanted me and Stefano to get to know each other? They were building more hotels?

I swallowed as I set my plate down on the side table next to me. I wasn't hungry anymore. Not only had Dad told me I needed to spend the summer with the Espositos, he was basically telling me that my future was set with this announcement.

And my future included Stefano.

"Did you know about this?" Jet asked, turning to look at me.

I hated the tears that filled my lids as I shook my head. I didn't want to cry in front of Jet. I didn't want to cry because my parents didn't care that I didn't want the life they'd planned for me.

And I didn't want to feel as weak as I felt right now.

"I need to go to the bathroom," I whispered as I stood and rushed down the hall that jutted off from the living room.

Thankfully, Jet called out, "Second door on the left," before I had to go back and ask them where it was.

Once I was in the safety of the bathroom, I shut the door and collapsed against it. Tears streamed down my cheeks as

I tipped my face up toward the ceiling.

Why was I crying? I wasn't a baby. Besides, it wasn't like I didn't know this was happening. I'd been sitting at the table this morning. I'd guessed their plan.

I'd just figured that maybe there was a chance they could change their mind.

But that press conference had felt definite. This was happening whether I was on board or not. Dad didn't get into business with someone on a whim. They'd been planning this for a while.

Which meant I'd been a part of this plan for a while. And Mom and Dad had waited until there was no time for me to even try to change their minds.

My future was set.

Frustrated about the tears I was shedding, I walked over to the toilet and sat down. I reached over and grabbed some toilet paper and began blotting my cheeks. I was such a loser right now.

What kind of girl turns down a handsome foreigner and a chance to spend a summer in an exotic country? Most girls would be throwing themselves at Stefano instead of running away.

I sighed, thankful the tears had subsided. I hated how out of control I felt when I cried. I could hear Dad's annoyed voice in my mind. "No good ever came from blubbering," he'd tell me whenever I was sad or frustrated.

And maybe that was true. Crying did nothing to change my circumstance. So why waste the energy?

After I gathered some control over my emotions, I stood

and glanced at myself in the mirror. My eyes were puffy and my cheeks were pink. I turned on the water and let the cool temperature shock my system. I splashed my face a few times and then grabbed a towel and dried off.

That seemed to help me look less like a mess and a little more in control. I unlocked the bathroom door and made my way out to the hall, where I heard a voice I didn't recognize. It was female and it sounded as if she were celebrating.

"That's great, Brit," Jet said.

I made my way into the living room and saw a girl who was a few inches shorter than Jet. She was wearing the same light-blue Livingstone Hotel uniform as Jet's mom. Her hands were clasped together.

"I can't believe it. Hank said I'm next in line for shift manager once the new hotels open." She collapsed on the couch and rested her hand on her forehead. From the slump of her shoulders, I could tell she was just as exhausted as her mom.

"It's amazing!" Cassidy said as she climbed across the couch and snuggled in next to her.

Brit wrapped her arm around Cassidy and pulled her close. "Thanks, sweetie." She glanced up to Jet. "This means big things for us."

I glanced over to watch Jet's reaction, and the slow smile that spread across his lips told me everything I needed to know. A merger between the Espositos and Livingstones meant good things for a lot of people.

My whole body went numb as the realization of what that meant for my future settled around me.

My parents had played my hand. I was stuck. No matter how much my feelings for Jet were beginning to grow, it didn't matter.

My future was set.

And my future included Stefano.

CHAPTER TEN

I slunk over to the corner to lean against the wall, hoping it would help hold me up. The pain that coursed through my body felt as real as the pain of having an arm cut off. Or stubbing a toe.

My life was irreversibly changed, no matter how much I wanted it to be different.

"Who's your friend, Jet?" Brit's words sounded in my ears, but I just couldn't bring myself to look up at her.

Jet appeared in front of me. His forehead was furrowed. "You okay? You look pale."

I nodded as I stepped out from under his scrutiny. "I'm fine. I just...I left something in the bathroom."

"Oh, okay," Brit said, giving me a smile that just made me feel worse.

I nodded and scurried past her. Once I was in the hall, I kept my gaze on the ground until I was back in the bathroom.

I collapsed against the door. What was I doing here? What was wrong with me? I shook my head as I closed my eyes tight. I'm not sure what I thought I would accomplish by slinking away. It wasn't like I was in the magical land of Oz where all I had to do was click my heels and wish for everything to be okay.

My life wasn't a fairytale. It was real. My problems were real, and my decisions could affect a lot of people.

Thanks for stacking on the guilt, Mom and Dad.

I blew out my breath and headed over to the sink. I felt like an idiot, hiding in the bathroom again. But what else could I do? I didn't live here. Where else was I supposed to go to throw my tantrum?

In the mirror, my normally bright blue eyes looked as stormy as my soul felt. I wasn't sure what I was going to do. I didn't want to go to Italy. I wanted nothing to do with Stefano. And yet, I knew I couldn't disappoint so many people who were depending on our families' merger.

There was so much more at stake now that my feelings for Jet were growing. Why had I thought I could have a weekend away? My decisions would follow me whether I liked it or not.

"Stupid," I whispered under my breath.

I wished I could say that I would take this whole weekend back. That I'd click my heels and return to the time right before I got on Jet's stupid motorcycle. Before I'd allowed myself to care for him. I would force myself to stay at the table and play nice with Stefano just like my parents wanted me to. I would have never left.

At least then I'd have a choice. I could have decided to help my parents or demand they stop meddling in my life. But now? How could I not go along with my parents' plan?

For some reason, leaving Jet in this situation when he had a chance to get out of it, made my heart hurt.

I patted my cheeks—maybe a bit too hard—and made my way over to the door. I swung it open and yelped.

Standing on the other side, leaning his shoulder on the door frame, was Jet. He glanced at me with a concerned look on his face.

"Everything okay?" he asked.

I forced a smile. "Yes. Of course. Why wouldn't it be?"

He straightened as he shoved his hands into his front pockets and shrugged. "You left before you could meet Brit." He met my gaze again. "Are you sure everything's okay?"

I patted his shoulder, ignoring the dull ache that rushed up my arm from the desire to touch him longer. "I'm just fine. Peachy keen."

He squinted. "Oh man, I don't think anyone but my grandma says that."

I dropped my hand. I couldn't keep touching him. It was beginning to mean too much to me. I needed to create more space between us. He needed to stay as far away from me as possible. I wasn't sure what I was going to do, and I couldn't disappoint him like that. He deserved better.

"Are you saying I'm a seventy-five-year-old woman?" I narrowed my eyes.

His gaze swept over me, and my skin heated from his

scrutiny. He quirked his eyebrow and shook his head. "Definitely not a seventy-five-year-old woman."

I stared at him, and the butterflies in my stomach multiplied by the second. Was he flirting with me? Did I dare hope?

Before I allowed myself to fall into the black hole that was deciphering Jet's intentions, I shrugged and passed by him. I ignored the feeling that exploded through my body as my arm brushed his abs.

He wasn't for me. We couldn't be anything.

"Well, I'm glad we got that covered," I said as I made my way down the hall toward the kitchen, where I could hear Brit and Cassidy talking.

The sound of Jet's footsteps followed after me. I tried not to read into it. After all, he was probably just wanting to talk to his sisters.

Reading into anything he did was a mistake I couldn't allow myself to make. I needed to make sure that Jet stayed away from me. His future and the future of his family was controlled by my family, and I couldn't take that responsibility lightly.

Especially when I was pretty sure I was falling for him.

When I walked into the kitchen, I found Brit standing next to the counter, with a plate of fried chicken in her hands. She was smiling at Cassidy, who was sitting on the counter next to her. Brit's gaze roamed over me, and I saw the spark of recognition in her gaze.

"You're the Livingstone daughter," she said as she set the

plate down, brushed her hands against each other, and then made her way over to me.

"Brielle," I said as I took her hand.

"Brielle. That's right." She held my hand for a second before letting it go. She was peering into my eyes, and I could see the similarities between her and Jet. They both had deep green eyes and the same dark hair. Brit wore hers up in a ponytail. Wispy curls framed her face and caught the setting summer sun as it flowed in from the window.

Not sure what else I was supposed to say, I entwined my fingers and rested my hands in front of me. When people learned who I was—especially if they worked for my parents—they'd suddenly start airing all of their grievances with my parents to me. Like there was something I could do about it.

And trust me, if I could, I would.

"Are you enjoying your time at home?" she asked. Her smile felt warm and inviting, and I wasn't sure how to take it.

I nodded. "It's normal."

Her gaze flicked over to Jet and then back to me. "I didn't know you knew Jet."

Jet shrugged as he walked over to the fridge and pulled out a soda. The sound of the pressure being released filled the kitchen. "We just met. I'm showing her around Atlantic City."

"Well isn't that nice of you."

Jet shrugged as he tipped the can to his lips. When he

finished, he swallowed and wiped his mouth. "I'm nothing if not chivalrous."

Brit snorted and shook her head. "Not where I was going with that."

Jet must have drained the can with his second drink because he crumpled the can in his hand and threw it into the garbage can. "It's okay. I said it for you."

The sound of the backdoor opening halted any further conversation. All of us turned to see Jet's dad stumble into the kitchen.

The atmosphere in the room suddenly turned chilly as Brit and Jet straightened and glanced at each other. They must have some secret form of communication because they both nodded as Brit stepped forward and hoisted Cassidy off the counter.

"Go with Brit," Jet hissed as he stepped closer to me. Then he turned so his back was to me. Like he was shielding me.

For a moment, I thought about protesting, but when I glanced over at Brit and saw the pleading look in her eyes, I decided to comply.

She quickened her step as she kept one hand on Cassidy's head and the other holding Cassidy against her body. Brit made her way through the hallway and into the back room. I followed closely behind her. Once we both cleared the room, she shut the door. Muffled yelling could be heard from the kitchen.

My stomach squeezed as I could make out bits and pieces of what was being said.

Jet's dad was upset that everyone had left. Then his anger turned toward Jet pulling him out of the casino this morning. As Mr. Miller's voice grew louder and more menacing, my whole body felt heavy. I hated how Mr. Miller was talking to Jet. It felt almost as if he was saying those things to me.

"Hey, you okay?" Brit asked.

I hadn't realized that I'd camped out next to the door until I looked up. I had to be in Cassidy and Brit's room because it was decked out in pink. A bunkbed sat alongside the far wall. Cassidy was peering down at me from the top. She held a monkey stuffed animal over her head as if she were trying to cover her ears.

I glanced back at Brit to see that her expression looked as solemn as I felt.

"Is he going to be okay?" I asked, nodding toward the kitchen.

Brit glanced over at Cassidy and then back to me. She smiled, but I could see that it was fake. Which made my stomach drop. No. This wasn't going to end well.

"They'll be fine. Jet knows what to do," she said as she wrapped her arms around her chest and assumed a protective stance.

I studied her. I felt so helpless standing here, listening to the anger carrying down the hall from the kitchen. I wondered how many times Jet had stood out there, taking the brunt of his dad's anger. How many times he'd protected his sisters.

Anger built up inside of me. The fact that Jet's dad

treated his son like this... Heat pricked my body. It was taking all of my strength not to open the door, stomp down the hall, and give the man a piece of my mind.

If I thought it might help, I would do it. But I doubted Jet would see it as a heroic gesture. Plus, I didn't want to make things worse. So I sat there, listening to the yelling.

"Let's turn on some music," Brit said, walking over to the boombox that sat on the dresser.

The scratchy sound of the DJ drowned out the voices, so I leaned against the door to hear better.

Worry. Fear. Pain. All of these feelings were coursing through my body and constricting my throat until I felt as if I couldn't breathe.

Was Jet okay? What was happening?

I knew things weren't good. From the strained look on Brit's face, I could tell she knew what Jet was going through. Her fingers were pressing pretty hard into her arm as she kept them crossed in front of her chest.

I needed to know what was happening. I needed her to confirm that things weren't as bad as I was imagining. But I needed to get Brit away from Cassidy to ask her.

"Brit," I whispered, leaning toward her and hoping she could hear me.

Brit glanced over, and I motioned for her to come closer. She gave me a wide smile as she glanced over at Cassidy and then back to me. Thankfully, Cassidy had lain back in her bed, and all we could see was her bouncing foot that kept time with the beat.

Brit seemed to take that as her chance, so she quietly made her way over to where I stood.

"What?" she asked. Her tone was short and curt.

I pretended not to notice. "Is he okay?" I asked, nodding in the direction of the kitchen.

Brit followed my gesture and then glanced back at me. She chewed her lip like she was working up the nerve to talk. "I..." She shook her head as she dropped her gaze. "There's something you need to know about Jet."

I nodded as I leaned in closer. My heart hammered in my chest. I wanted to know everything about Jet.

"What?"

She glanced up. "He'll do anything for the people he loves." She rubbed the back of her neck and then touched her lip as if she were remembering something. "He'd take away the pain of the people he loves if he could." She glanced over to Cassidy and then back to me. "He'll protect us no matter the cost."

My stomach plummeted to the floor. That was my fear. Suddenly, my heart broke for Jet. Hadn't I already witnessed this sort of self-sacrifice with Crew? With Cassidy?

I glanced back at the door. I wanted to leave. I wanted to run into the kitchen and be that protection for Jet. More than I'd wanted to do anything else in my entire life. "We should help him," I said under my breath, not really meaning for Brit to hear.

She placed her palm against the wood of the door. "No. It will only make things worse. We stay here until he comes to get us." I could see the tears brimming in her eyes as I glanced over at her. "It's his rule."

I wanted to push her aside. I wanted to run to Jet. To protect him. But from the desperation in her gaze, I knew I shouldn't. I needed to stay rooted to this spot. If that was his wish, I'd give it to him.

It was sheer torture standing there next to the door, willing it to open. I kept leaning toward it, straining to hear if he was coming down the hall. But all I could hear was the faint sound of voices until there was nothing. No sound.

I folded my arms and tipped my head up as I leaned against the wall. I closed my eyes and thought about Jet.

I thought about what he was doing for Brit. For his family. How selfless he was.

And suddenly, I felt horrible. Here I was, complaining about the fact that my family was trying to take care of me in the best—albeit barbaric—way they knew how.

I mean, sure, my parents wanted to marry me off to cement a business partnership, but at least they didn't abuse me. Or force me to protect other people in my life from them.

I was acting like a selfish brat.

Ugh. I disliked myself a lot right now.

And the fact that I kept questioning if I should go to Italy or not, even though it was pretty obvious that going would help Jet's family, made me feel even worse.

I was a terrible person.

I tipped my head forward and studied Brit and Cassidy.

Brit had made her way up into Cassidy's bed, and all I

could see were the tips of their toes and the soft melody of their voices.

An overwhelming desire to protect them—to protect Jet —came over me. Even though we'd just met, I cared about him. I wanted to see him happy. I needed him to be.

That was why, when this weekend was over, I was leaving for Italy.

I was going to do whatever it took to make sure the deal between the Espositos and Livingstones took place. It was the least I could do.

After all, if this was my final hurrah, I might as well go out with a bang.

Footsteps came down the hallway, and I straightened and peered over at the door. I tried to calm my nerves as I watched the handle turn and the crack between the door and the frame widen.

"He's gone," Jet's low voice said from the hall. He had his face dipped down, and even though I couldn't see it, I knew something was wrong.

He avoided my gaze as he turned and made his way down the hall and into the bathroom. I followed after him, recognizing that retreat. I'd made it so many times in the past.

"Jet," I said, reaching out to grab his elbow.

He hesitated but kept his face hidden. "Let me go, Brielle."

I shook my head, fearing the worst. I wasn't going to let him go. I couldn't. I was here for him. I needed to be needed.

"Please. Let me see."

For a moment, I thought he was going to look up. I thought he was going to let me in. Instead, he ducked past me and into the bathroom, where he shut the door.

Rage and anger coursed through me as I grabbed the door handle and turned. Thankfully, I seemed to have caught him right before he locked the door. I pushed the door open.

That must have thrown Jet off guard because I was suddenly staring at his very bloody, surprised face.

My body went numb as I stared at the broken skin across his cheekbone and his bleeding lip. His eye had begun to swell, but he still mustered an annoyed look.

"Brielle, what are you doing?"

I forced myself to put aside my fear and be there for him. Before he could push me out the door, I moved past him and over to the tub. I folded my arms. "I'm helping. You're not going to do this alone."

He studied me, and then he sighed. He glanced into the hallway to check if anyone was around and then shut and locked the door. He turned back to me, clearly frustrated.

"I have no say?" he asked.

I shook my head.

And that was the truth. We were friends. I was going to be there for him whether he liked it or not.

CHAPTER ELEVEN

*N*ow that I was locked in the bathroom with Jet, I began to wonder if I'd made the right choice. After all, I was supposed to be fighting my feelings for him, not putting myself in situations that would bring us closer to each other emotionally and physically.

This bathroom was tiny, so I couldn't avoid brushing against him. But Jet didn't seem to notice our predicament. He stood in front of the vanity, staring in the mirror. He leaned forward and gingerly touched his face. He must have gotten close to the cut because he winced as he dropped his hand.

I moved closer to him. "Sit," I said, pointing to the toilet.

Jet glanced over at me. "What?"

"Sit," I repeated. "I'm at least going to help you."

He raised his eyebrows. "Are you a nurse?"

I shook my head. "No. But I've been to a few parties that ended with guys being stupid."

He chuckled as he moved over to the toilet and sat down. He glanced up at me. "I'm not going to lie, I kind of want to see that."

"Me at a party?"

He nodded. "I have a hard time believing that you live this deviant life." His tone was low and a tad mocking.

I dropped my jaw. "Yeah, well, I'll have you know I've been known to paint the town."

His chuckle turned into a laugh. His wide smile caused him to wince and gingerly touch his cheek.

"Serves you right," I said, sticking my tongue out at him.

His laugh subsided. A thick silence fell around us, and for a moment, I wanted to go back to the laughter. At least then there wasn't any of this mystery about what he was feeling.

"Washcloth," I said, needing to busy myself.

Jet pointed to the cupboard above him. I nodded and then leaned over him to open one of the doors.

That was a mistake. Suddenly, I found myself inches away from Jet. I could feel his breath against my skin, and I felt his gaze on me as he glanced up.

And, stupid me, I glanced down to meet his gaze.

My stomach lightened as I stared into his eyes. They were dark and stormy, like he was holding onto something that was physically hurting him. And I had a pretty good idea what it was.

His dad.

"I'm sorry," I whispered.

His brow furrowed. "For what?"

I swallowed as I turned my attention back to the cupboard and pulled out a clean washcloth. Tears were building up in my eyes and I didn't want to lose what little control I had over my emotions. I feared that if I let the dam break, I was never going to be able to put it back.

With the washcloth in hand, I turned on the water and waited for it to turn warm.

"It's not your fault," Jet said, his voice breaking through my thoughts.

I glanced over at him to see his expression had softened as he studied me.

I nodded as I rung out the soaking wet washcloth and walked the two steps over to him. I hated that I was making him feel like he needed to comfort me. He was the one that had been hurt, not me. And yet, he was taking care of me, like that was his job.

I wanted to actually do something for him, so I pushed out my feelings as I zeroed in on his cuts. "This might sting."

Jet shrugged. "I'm tough."

I nodded. "I know."

I hated how intently he was studying me as I began to dab the washcloth against his skin. He winced a few times as I brushed the material over the open wound, but that was it. He was stoic the rest of the time.

What was he thinking? My entire body burned with curiosity.

Was he feeling things too or was it only me?

"Are you enjoying your weekend?" he asked.

Relieved to be talking about something besides my feelings, I nodded. "Yeah. It's been eventful. A lot more exciting than what I'm used to."

Jet folded his arms. "I find that hard to believe. Why would someone want to slum it with me when they're used to caviar and cocktail parties?"

I shook my head. "That's not me. That's my parents. They care about that kind of stuff. I just want..." My voice broke, and suddenly I felt weak and vulnerable. I wasn't sure if I was okay with opening myself up to Jet like that. Because if I did, I wasn't ever going to be able to take it back.

And I was leaving on Sunday. I knew that. Keeping myself guarded was the only way I would get through boarding that airplane for Italy. The only way I was going to be able to accomplish whatever my family needed me to do so that this deal went through.

My relationship with Jet wasn't part of that deal. It had no place in my future.

But when he reached up and wrapped his hand around my wrist, the warmth that filled my soul sent shivers through my body. I could feel his eyes on me as he waited for me to acknowledge him.

There was this pull inside of me. On the one hand, I wanted to look. I wanted to dive headfirst into my feelings for Jet. I wanted to care for him in a raw and unabashed way. But the other part of me, the part that was trying to protect my heart, was telling me not to look. Because I knew once I did, there was no going back.

I was falling hard for Jet.

"Brielle," he said. His voice was deep and full of tension. It sent pulses of pleasure throughout my body. The part of me that wanted to meet his gaze was winning out. My resolve to keep my distance seemed foolish and ridiculous.

What would looking at him hurt?

"Yes?" I asked, keeping my eyes trained on his hand.

"Look at me."

I pinched my lips together as I shook my head. "I can't."

His other hand appeared in my line of sight as he rested his finger under my chin. He applied soft pressure, guiding my gaze up to meet his.

And when I looked into his eyes, all my worry, all my fear, subsided.

"What do you want?" he asked.

I swallowed back the emotions that were exploding inside of me. I held his gaze like he was a life raft and I was drowning. I wasn't sure how to articulate exactly what I wanted. How does one say that they want their parents to care about them enough to pay attention to them. To care for them enough to not force them into a relationship their child hadn't chosen?

How does someone say that they've felt lonely their entire life, even though they'd always been surrounded by people?

And then I knew. I knew what I'd been looking for. What I wanted.

"To be loved." My voice broke as I held his gaze.

His expression stilled as he studied me. Suddenly, he was

standing. His finger still pressed against my chin as if he feared that I'd back away.

And I'm not going to lie, that thought had crossed my mind.

But, as he stood there staring down at me, his warmth washing over me, all I wanted to do was lean in. To fall into Jet. To care for him in all the ways I'd been wanting someone to care for me.

He dropped my wrist and, with his now free hand, wrapped his arm around my waist, pulling me closer. He leaned into me, his lips inches from mine.

I could feel his breath grow heavy and his heart pick up speed as I sprawled my hands against his chest. Even though we'd kissed earlier today, this felt different.

This had meaning in it. Intention.

I could feel his struggle as he fought this primal desire to kiss me. It was just like the one going on inside of me. The desire to kiss weighed against the need to protect ourselves.

A staccato knock sounded on the door, causing Jet and I to jump apart. I dropped my hands to my side as Jet pushed his through his hair and sat back down on the toilet.

I swallowed back all the feelings that had woken in my soul from being held by him. In a desperate desire to distract myself, I turned the water back on and ran it over the washcloth.

"Who is it?" Jet asked, his voice startling me.

I forced myself to calm down. I needed to be better at keeping him at a distance, or I was doomed.

"Cassidy," she said.

I glanced over at him, and I could see the worry etched on his features. He shook his head and I nodded, knowing exactly how he felt. He didn't want Cassidy to see him like this, and I didn't blame him.

I held up my hand as I turned to the door and unlocked it. Then I pulled it open a few inches so she could barely see into the bathroom.

"He'll be a minute, sweetie."

Cassidy's eyebrows were drawn together and I could see her chin quivering as she tried to look inside. "Is Jet okay?"

I gave her my calmest smile. "He's great. Just a little cut, that's all. I'm going to fix him up and he'll be out in no time."

She glanced up at me and I could see the worry in her gaze.

"Do you know what would help him feel better?" I said.

She nodded, tears brimming her lids.

"A picture. Of you two." I steadied my gaze and widened my eyes. "Do you think you could do that?"

Her forehead creased, and then she nodded. "Yes."

I reached around the door and gave her a high-five. "By the time you're done, he'll be out."

She smiled, and before I could say anything else, she sprinted down the hallway to her room.

With her gone, I returned to Jet, shutting the door softly behind me. I glanced over to see him studying me. I forced down the butterflies that had decided to wake up inside my stomach and returned to the faucet.

Once the washcloth was ready, I continued to wash the cuts on Jet's face. Thankfully, he didn't push me to talk again. I worked in silence, cleaning the cuts and then applying antibiotic cream.

I offered to put on a princess bandage, but he held up his hand.

"I'm good," he said.

I shrugged as I put everything away. Jet stood and glanced into the mirror, turning his face from one side to the next.

"Nice job, Blondie," he said, glancing over at me and winking.

I rolled my eyes, making sure he understood my meaning. "Really?"

He shrugged as his hand fell to his shirt, where some blood had dropped. Suddenly, he was pulling his shirt off over his head.

I stood there, staring at his incredibly toned and tanned body. I mean, I knew there were muscles under his shirt—I'd felt them whenever I'd been pressed against him—but there was definitely something different about staring at them.

His chuckle drew me from my trance, and heat rushed across my skin to settle in my cheeks.

"You okay?" he asked with a light, mocking tone to his voice. He held his shirt in his hands. "You're looking a bit flushed."

I glared at him as I folded my arms. "You couldn't wait until you were in your room"—I waved my hand toward his chest—"to do that?"

His gaze darted around the bathroom. "People normally take their shirts off in the bathroom, do they not?"

I could literally feel my body temperature rising, but I wasn't going to let him win this. "Yes."

He motioned to the walls around us. "And we are in the bathroom, right?"

I shook my head. "Still, how would you like it if I started removing my clothes?" I clamped my mouth shut. My body was on fire now. Why was I still talking?

Jet shrugged. "I'll do what I've gotta do. You do what you've gotta do."

I growled as I started pushing him toward the door. "It's time for you to go."

He protested, pushing himself back into the bathroom. "May I remind you that you were the one who followed me in here."

I shook my head as I pushed against his arm. "I need a moment."

He slowly started moving toward the door. "If I didn't know better, I'd think you were trying to get rid of me."

I nodded. "Great. Then my plan is working. I am trying to get rid of you."

He stopped and dropped his gaze down to meet mine. "Ouch. And here I thought we were becoming friends."

Exasperated, I dropped my hands and glared at him. "We won't be if you don't let me pee."

He chuckled as he reached out and grabbed the door handle. He swept his gaze over me, causing my heart to beat harder and faster than it had ever done. If Jet didn't leave now, he'd realize just how hard it was for me to keep my distance. He'd discover what I was really trying hard to fight.

I was falling for him.

Hard.

His gaze met mine, and he held it for a moment. Then he sighed as he turned the handle and pulled open the door. I almost let out my breath as he stepped out into the hall, but then he turned, resting his arms on either side of the doorway. "Thanks for cleaning me up," he said. The smile that emerged on his lips just about turned my knees to jelly.

I nodded. "Anytime."

He paused and then allowed me to shut the door. I collapsed on the toilet, grateful to give my body a break. It took a lot of control to fight my feelings for Jet, and I was exhausted.

I tipped my head back and closed my eyes. My heart was still racing, and my cheeks were burning from the memory of Jet so close to me. I shook my head.

Why did I think it would be smart to get into a tiny bathroom with him? Did I have a death wish?

I chewed my lip as I straightened. I needed a distraction. Something to pull me out of this confusing mess I'd put myself in. After all, how did I think I could do this? Would keeping away from Jet be enough to not break my heart when I left?

That was stupid. There was no way I was going to come out of this weekend unscathed.

Perhaps it was time to pull the ripcord. Get out of this

before I broke my already cracking heart. If I got away from Jet now, he'd be safe and so would I.

If I got any deeper, there would be no way I could get onto the plane Monday morning and save his sister's promotion. If I cared about him, I needed to leave.

I stared at Kate's number, knowing what I needed to do. I'd call her and get this whole dumb decision behind me.

I found her number, brought the speaker up to my ear, and waited. Two rings and Kate answered.

"Hey, girl. What's up?"

Tears welled up inside of me, but I wasn't going to cry now. I needed to be strong. "I was wondering if I could spend the weekend with you."

I could hear her snapping her gum on the other end. "Sure. Why?"

I sighed. "My parents are shipping me off to Italy with the Espositos. I think they want me to marry their son as some part of their business deal."

Kate laughed. "What? Are they crazy?"

I nodded. "Yeah, I'm pretty sure they are. Anyway, I want to get away. Could you come pick me up?"

"Sure. I'm about ten minutes from the Livingstone."

I winced as I closed my eyes. I needed to prepare myself for Kate's over-the-top reaction to what I was about to tell her. "I'm not exactly there."

"Okay, where are you?"

"Do you know a Jet Miller?"

All I could hear after that was screaming. Like, ear-piercing, dogs would join in, type of screaming. It went on for a good ten seconds before she had to catch her breath and I could speak.

"I'm assuming you know him."

"Yeah, I know him. He was like the rebel of the school last year." She took a deep breath. "How do you know him, and why are you with him?"

I took a deep breath. I really didn't want to get into it over the phone. "It doesn't matter. I'll tell you once you're here. Can you just come get me?"

"Yeah. I'll be there in ten."

"Do you know where he lives?"

"Oh, honey, everyone knows where Jet lives."

We said our goodbyes, and, once the phone fell silent, I set it on the counter next to me. I was trying to fight the twinge of sadness that had settled in my chest. I knew I should be happy; I was sparing myself and Jet from the inevitable heartbreak that would take place if he and I actually allowed ourselves to grow close.

I was protecting myself as well as him.

Even though my stomach was tying itself in knots and my heart felt as if it were crumbling to pieces, I knew this was for the best.

It was the only way for Jet to be happy, and that was all that mattered to me.

CHAPTER TWELVE

$\mathcal{I}$ tried to stay in the bathroom until Kate got there, but Cassidy wasn't having it. She kept knocking and trying to whisper into the crack of the door. When she asked me if I needed medicine, I decided it was best to get out of the bathroom. No reason to make people think I had bowel issues or something.

Jet was in the kitchen with his hands elbow-deep in sudsy water when I walked in. He'd put on a shirt and looked so adorable standing there washing dishes that I almost turned around and ran back into the bathroom, not caring what anyone assumed about my bathroom needs.

All I could think about as I stood there, dumbfounded, was how much I liked Jet. Like, really liked him.

And the more I was around him, the harder I was falling for him.

He must have heard me come in because he turned and

winked at me. "What? Never seen a guy do the dishes before?" he asked.

His half smile made my knees feel as if they were going to collapse. My whole body was responding to the way his gaze swept over me and the look in his eyes as he met mine.

I scoffed, hoping that I would come across as cool instead of the nerd I felt like. "I've seen guys do the dishes before," I said as I walked over to the oven, grabbed a towel, and began drying the stack of dishes that he was piling up next to him.

"Thanks," he said as I took a plate from him.

The sound of his voice and the way he leaned into me caused shivers to cascade down my back. Before I could police myself, my fingers brushed his and I almost dropped the dish.

Jet's soapy hands were suddenly on mine as he tried to grab the plate. His laugh was soft, and I felt him glance over at me. Heat pricked at the back of my neck, but I kept my gaze trained on the plate.

"Sorry," I whispered.

Jet let go of the dish and stepped back to grab another dish. I hoped that really was reason, and not just an opportunity to get away from me. He dunked the next dish into the water and started scrubbing.

We worked in silence. I kept my ears open for the sound of Kate's arrival. I wanted to get away and to stay at the same time. It was exhausting to have such conflicting feelings raging inside of me.

I just knew that if I could just get away from Jet, maybe I could actually figure out what I wanted. Or how I was going to end this weekend without my heart shredded to bits.

"You okay?" he asked as he dipped down, trying to catch my gaze.

I pinched my lips together as I snapped my attention back to the dish I was drying. "Yes," I whispered.

He stopped moving and turned to face me. I could see him stare from the corner of my eye. What was he thinking, and why was he looking at me like that?

"He's not going to come back. He never does. He'll probably go sleep it off at his friend's or another bar."

Confused, I glanced over at him, only to have my breath taken away. Jet had this soulful, worried look in his eyes. Like he was concerned about me.

"Who?" I asked.

He blinked a few times. "My dad," he said slowly.

Right. "Oh. Okay," I replied.

"Was that not who you were waiting for?" He returned to the sink and sunk his hands back into the water.

I shook my head. "No."

He glanced over at me. "Then why do you keep looking over at the door?"

I took in a deep breath and then let it out slowly. It made a soft whistling sound. "I asked my friend Kate to come pick me up."

I wasn't sure what I'd expected Jet to do when I finally confessed that I'd asked Kate to come get me, but the frustrated expression on his face surprised me.

He looked angry.

I'd figured I was doing him a favor. Leaving before he and I started down a path we couldn't finish. And maybe if he knew about Italy, he'd be fine with it. But that was a secret I couldn't bring myself to tell him. I didn't want him to see me as this weak girl who just did whatever her parents told her to do.

Sure, I always ended up giving my parents what they wanted. It was easier to give in than try to battle a Livingstone, but right now, I didn't want Jet to look at me with pity in his eyes. It felt harder to live with than just anger.

"Why?" he asked as he plopped a pan covered in grease into the sink, causing soap bubbles to shoot into the air. "If it's about my dad, he's gone. I promise. He won't be coming back until he sobers up."

My emotions were choking my throat. So many thoughts, so many feelings, were coursing through me, and I wasn't sure how to handle any of them. Pushing them way down felt like the best option. At least until I was no longer around Jet.

I could hold out until I was gone as long as I got some distance between us.

"It's not about your dad," I said as I wiped the plate I was drying. I needed something semi-normal to focus on, and wiping a plate gave that to me.

"So, what? Haven't I delivered what you asked for?"

I peeked over at him and saw that he'd placed both hands on the front of the sink and was leaning in so that his shoulders were pushed up to his ears. I couldn't tell he was frustrated from looking at him, but I could hear it in his voice.

"You've been great. Really. I just..." I sighed. I didn't want to hurt him, but I also didn't want him to think that there was a chance I would stay.

Because I would, if he asked.

Deep down, I didn't want to go. I wanted to stay here. I wanted to be with Jet.

Only, I couldn't have him. It would never work.

My parents would never allow me to date him. And if I tried, it might compromise my parents' deal, and I couldn't do that to Jet's family. Too much was a stake, and my happiness seemed to get lost in it all.

"I just realized that maybe I was being a little childish and I should probably head back." I shrugged like what I was saying was not big deal...even though it was. A really big deal.

When he didn't say anything, I peered over at him, wondering what he was thinking. Did he hate me? Was he relieved? Sad?

I shook my head. I couldn't let myself get wrapped up in how he felt. I feared my lack of strength if he cared in the slightest that I was leaving. I feared that if he asked me to stay, I would. My resolve would crumble, and I'd lose all the strength that I'd gathered to get through this.

Before he could say anything, his phone rang. He pulled his hand from the sink and shook it off. Then he reached into his back pocket and pulled out his phone.

"Hello?"

I pretended to busy myself with the next dish. I wasn't trying to listen to the conversation, but it was hard not to.

"Hey, man, what are you up to?"

I was pretty sure it was Crew on the other end.

Jet glanced over at me, pulled his other hand out of the water, and shook it off as he made his way over to lean against the fridge.

"My evening just freed up. Why? Where are you?"

I tried not to wince at Jet's words or the bite to his tone. I'd hurt him. I could hear it in his voice, and it was getting harder and harder to convince myself it was for his good.

"Shut up and Drink? What time?"

I had no idea what he was talking about. I wanted to ask, but I knew it wasn't my business anymore.

"Thirty minutes?"

I saw Jet peer around the fridge. Then he moved back to lean on the fridge. "Yeah, I think I can make that work. Once things are wrapped up here, I'll head over."

He listened for a moment.

"Man, I told you. That's over. She's in the past."

More silence.

I felt like the room around me was shrinking. I wanted to know who he was talking about. Who was in the past? Was it an ex? Was she going to be there tonight?

I cleared my throat, just to get my own thoughts to shut up. I needed to stop thinking and just focus on getting out of there.

"Fine. Fine. It's okay. I'll come."

Jet didn't sound too pleased about whatever Crew had said, but after he said his goodbyes and slipped his phone back into his pocket, he returned to the dishes like nothing had happened.

Here I was, standing next to him, feeling like I was going to burst with questions. I chewed my lip in an effort to give myself something to do other than talk. I shouldn't care what Jet did or who he was seeing tonight. I was done with him.

I had to be.

I finished drying the last dish while Jet unplugged the sink and rinsed the remaining soap down the drain. Just as I tucked the towel around the oven handle, there was an erratic knock on the door.

Kate.

Relief flooded my body as I headed over to the door, but Jet beat me to it. He pulled the door open, and I could see the huge smile that emerged.

"Kate Wilson. What are you doing here?"

The laugh that escaped Kate's lips made me wince. She was anything but stealth. Even I could read her emotions.

"Jet Miller. It's good to see you," she said amidst her giggles.

"Come in," he said, pushing the door open farther and nodding toward the kitchen.

"Thanks," she said as she entered. When she saw me, she squealed and rushed over to me and gave me a huge hug. "I'm so happy you're back," she said.

I didn't want to let go of her. With the way I was feeling, I needed to hold onto everything that brought me peace. And right there and then, that was Kate.

If Kate noticed my clinginess, she didn't say anything about it. Instead, she gave me a smile before she turned back to Jet. "I love your kitchen," she said as she peered around at the yellow wallpaper.

Jet snorted. "Right," he said. He was leaning against the counter, and he had this sort of cocky arrogance about him. Like he'd won something, but I wasn't quite sure what. And I wasn't sure I wanted to know.

Kate's cheeks hinted pink as she giggled. "It gets the job done, am I right?"

I stared at my friend, who couldn't hide her gushing feelings for Jet. I knew if I didn't get her out of there, she was going to be a big puddle of goo on the floor with the words Jet Miller imprinted on her.

"Come on," I said, linking arms with her and pulling her toward the door. "We should get going. Jet's got plans for the night, and we don't want to be rude."

As soon as those words left my lips, regret filled me. I pinched my lips together so that nothing else could escape and pulled at her arm again.

Kate would not be deterred, however. She ignored me and turned to Jet. "Plans? What plans do you have?"

Jet's smile made me wince. I hated how confident he seemed as he pushed off the counter and shoved his hands into his front pockets. "Oh, just meeting some friends at

Shut Up and Drink." His gaze roamed over Kate before it landed on me. "Do you want to come?"

Yep. That's what I'd feared.

"I don't—"

"We'd love to come," Kate said.

I snapped my gaze over to Kate and gave her my best exasperated look. "We—"

"We can go," Kate said as she glanced between me and Jet.

"I really think Jet just wants to be with his friends," I said, leaning in to her. For my best friend, she was really bad at picking up on my hints.

"I don't mind. The more the merrier."

I tried not to glare at Jet as I met his gaze. "Yes, but it's your friends. I'm sure you want to be alone with them." My voice came out strained.

Was no one capable of picking up on my body language?

Jet shrugged. "It's not a birthday party. It's a group of us hanging out at a bar. It's pretty relaxed. I'm sure there will be other people there. And I'm okay with that," he said as he leaned toward me. I couldn't help but melt under his stare as he focused it on me.

"See, he doesn't care," Kate said as she swatted my arm.

I glared at her. I didn't want to go. And I didn't want to go home. I wanted to be with Kate somewhere far, far away from Jet. And my attempt at freedom was rapidly slipping from my grasp.

"It's settled then," Jet said as he clapped his hands together. "We're meeting there in thirty minutes."

Kate's smile was huge as she nodded vigorously. "Amazing." Then she glanced over at me. "We can make that work, right?"

I shrugged. I wasn't being heard anyway. I doubted that even if I yelled "fire" anyone would listen. "Sure," I said.

Kate nodded. "Perfect." I felt her gaze roam over me. Before I could stop her, she said, "Let's go get you changed, and then we'll meet Jet at the bar."

That was the exact opposite of what I wanted to do. Curling up on Kate's bed in a pair of her fleece pajamas while eating chocolates and watching sappy chick flicks was what I wanted to do. What I didn't want to do was to go to her house so she could dress me up for a party I didn't want to go to.

But Kate didn't pick up on my obvious sighs or stares in her direction. Instead, she linked arms with me and pulled me toward the door. She opened it and ushered me onto the front stoop. "See you soon," she sang out just as she shut the door.

I followed her down the driveway. Just before I climbed into her car, I heard a knock on the living room window. Cassidy's earnest face came into view.

"Bye, Brielle," she said, her voice muffled from the glass. Her little hand was waving so vigorously that I couldn't help but wave back.

"Bye, Cassidy."

She smiled and saluted me before disappearing behind the couch.

When I turned back, I saw a very smug smile on my best friend's face. I furrowed my brow as I stared at her.

"What?"

She snorted as she opened the driver's door and climbed into her seat. "I didn't say anything."

I glared at her. "You were thinking something," I said as I sat on the passenger seat and buckled my seatbelt. Just as I shut my door, she started the engine and pulled away from the curb.

"I just think it's interesting that I find you at Jet Miller's house waving goodbye to his little sister." She paused at a stop sign and took that time to stare me down. "Is there something you want to tell me?"

The all-too-familiar lump returned to my throat as I fiddled with the hem of my dress. "No," I whispered.

I was so close to losing control of my emotions, and I feared talking about it would reopen the waterworks. I needed to be strong. I had to be.

When she didn't respond, I glanced up at her to see her studying the road.

"That's it?" I asked, kind of shocked that she didn't ask me any more questions. Kate was not one to give up so easily.

Kate shrugged. "I figure I have all night to get answers from you," she said, glancing over at me.

I nodded, relief rushing through me. I was grateful that she didn't press me, even though she was going to expect answers at some point. But maybe by then I could actually give them to her. Right then, I needed to wallow. I needed the comfort burying my feelings brought me.

Because once I broke that dam, I was going to be forever changed. And I wasn't sure I could handle that right now.

CHAPTER THIRTEEN

I stared at the black minidress that Kate picked out for me to wear. It was form-fitting and definitely not something I was used to wearing. My legs looked like they went on for days, especially when I wore a pair of stiletto heels with them.

"I'm not sure," I said, pulling down the hem of the skirt. I hoped it would do something. Maybe cover me up a tad bit more. But it didn't.

"What are you talking about? You look amazing. Jet's eyes are going to bug out."

I snapped my gaze to her, and a shush escaped my lips. That was the exact last thing I needed to happen. I'd only been apart from him for fifteen minutes, and I already missed him. How I had gone seventeen years without him in my life boggled my mind.

He'd changed me, and I wasn't sure I was ever going to change back.

"I don't care about that," I said as I reached up to unzip the dress. If that's what Kate truly thought about Jet's reaction, then there was no way I could wear this. I didn't want to go to the bar in the first place, and wearing a dress that would intrigue Jet was definitely not what I was going for.

"I'm joking," Kate said as she reached up and grasped my hands, making it impossible for me to take the dress off. "You look great in that. Don't change."

I wiggled my fingers and she let me go. I stared at my reflection before I sighed and dropped my hands. "Fine. After all, this is my final hurrah. I might as well make it count."

Kate stepped between me and the mirror. "What are you talking about, final hurrah?"

Right. She didn't know about Italy or Stefano. Or my most likely impending nuptials. "Never mind," I said as I let out my breath in a slow hiss. I wasn't in the mood to talk about any of this. I loved Kate, but I didn't need her freaking out and confusing me more than I already was.

When I glanced back at her and saw her folded arms and impatient gaze, I knew that an explanation was inevitable. So I took a deep breath and told her everything.

I told her about the Espositos. The merger. Stefano. Italy. I told her about Jet and the kiss we shared in the alleyway. I told her that what had started out as innocent fun had slowly turned into something more. And I was pretty sure I wasn't going to be able to get over it.

Kate didn't say much. Instead she stared at me, nodding her head as I talked through my issues. By the time I was finished, she was staring at me. Her lips were parted as if she was trying to figure out what to say but didn't know how to start.

I studied her, not sure if I wanted to hear her response. I was pretty sure there wasn't anything she could say that would make me feel better.

"Wow," she finally whispered.

I pinched my lips together and nodded.

She shook her head and then began pacing. "It's not fair. That's not cool. Your parents...they can't do this to you."

I shrugged. "Even if that was true, is that a risk I can take? I mean, the merger between the Espositos and the Livingstones would change Jet's family's life. I can't be responsible for taking that away. I would feel terrible." I sunk down onto the bed as I cradled my forehead in my hands.

I felt the bed shift as Kate sat down next to me.

"Listen to me. You have to tell Jet. He has to know why you're pulling away."

I glanced over at her, frustration filling me. "I can't. I mean, what if he tells me to stay. I don't think I have the strength to walk away. And I can't hurt his family." I closed my eyes as I pictured Brit's huge smile contrasted against Jet's bruised face.

If I could get them out of the poverty they were in, I was going to do it. Brit's better job depended on me upholding my end of the bargain.

"He deserves to know." She sucked in her breath. "I have

a feeling it wasn't me he wanted there tonight." Kate reached over and grabbed my hand. "I think it was you."

Tears stung my eyes as I stared at her. Was it true? Did I dare hope? My heart swelled at the thought, and I wanted to push it down. So far down that I couldn't feel anything.

But it wasn't letting me. I cared too much for Jet. I wanted to know if what Kate had said was true. Did he care about me?

It was so selfish of me to insert myself into his life just to find out if he cared for me the same way I did for him. But I knew I wouldn't be able to live with myself if I didn't ask him before I left.

"Kate..." I trailed off as emotions kept me from speaking.

She nodded as she patted my hand. "It's just a party. It'll be okay."

"Should I go?" I needed permission from an outsider. If she didn't think it made me a horrible person to go, then I could do it. I could force myself to stand and get into her car. I could force myself to see Jet again.

"Of course," she said as she stood and pulled me up. "You're going. You've got to stop living for your parents. If they are forcing you to do this, then you are going to party until you have to board that plane on Monday." She linked arms with me as we stared at our reflection in the mirror. "This weekend, you're going to make Brielle happy."

I turned to stare at her. Happy. Brielle and happy were two words that I hadn't associated with each other in a long time. I'd been satisfied with my life. Taken care of. But happy?

I shook my head. It wasn't until I met Jet that I'd finally allowed someone in. Allowed myself to be happy.

And I wanted to be happy for as long as possible.

I grabbed both of her hands and squeezed them. "Let's go," I said as adrenaline pumped through my veins.

"That's what I'm talking about," she squealed as she jumped up and down a few times. Then we opened the door and headed out of her room.

Once we were in the car and driving toward the bar, the confidence I had felt in her room had faded. As I stared out at the passing lights shining against the dark sky, I began to doubt the wisdom of what I was doing.

Was it fair to drag Jet into my mess? As much as I wanted to make myself happy, I couldn't help but wonder if it was worth sacrificing Jet's happiness. When I left for Italy, where would that leave Jet? If he did care about me, I doubted he would want me to leave on a plane with a guy my parents wanted me to date.

I wrapped my arms around my chest as regret washed over me. I wasn't being fair to Jet at all.

"I can't do this," I whispered as I glanced over at Kate.

She made a left and pulled into a packed parking lot. A building with bright neon lights on top of it that read "Shut up and Drink" was glowing in the darkness. People milled around outside. Some leaned against the building, smoking. Others were gathered in circles, laughing and just having a good time.

I shook my head. I shouldn't be here.

Kate's hand startled me into looking over at her. Her brows were furrowed as she studied me.

"It'll be okay, Brielle. Come on," she said as she pulled the keys from the ignition and got out.

I took a deep breath, hoping to dispel all the anxiety that had risen up in my chest, but it didn't help. I'd wanted to run away, and yet, I was walking into the exact situation I'd been trying to avoid.

The sound of our footsteps on the gravel reverberated in my ears as I followed Kate into the bar. A few guys made catcalls at us, but I was so focused on what I was going to say or do once I saw Jet that I didn't pay them any mind.

Once inside, Kate and I kept to the edges of the bar as we scouted the place. There was a group of kids who looked our age sitting at a table right next to a stage with a mic in the middle. It was as if they were waiting for something to happen.

Jet was half-sitting, half-standing at the table. His foot was propped up onto the chair in front of him. He had on his signature leather jacket, and I could practically smell it from where I stood. I guess all that time I spent with my arms wrapped around him on the back of his bike had cemented his scent into my mind.

"We should just go," I hissed, turning and grabbing Kate's arm.

She stumbled a bit when I took off toward the door, but she righted herself and halted my retreat. "Regret, Brielle. You can't have any if you're headed overseas."

I closed my eyes for a moment while I tried to gather all

the courage I could. She was right. If I was ever going to have a chance of getting over Jet, I needed to end it. Right here. Right now.

So I sucked in my breath and nodded. "Fine. Let's do this." I turned on my heel and headed toward Jet.

When I was a few feet from him, a girl with dark dreadlocks and a nose ring shot past me and wrapped her arms around Jet. Seeing her press her body against his made me stop. It was like I'd forgotten how to move. My feet felt rooted to the spot.

Jet's arm wrapped around her shoulder as he dipped down to listen to what she had to say. The other members of their group seemed to know who she was because they were all high-fiving her. She laughed as she threw her head back. Her perfectly long neck and smooth skin made me want to crawl into a dark corner and weep.

"Hey, it's Reality TV," Crew's voice pushed through the fog that coated my brain.

A second later, I registered his heavy arm on my shoulders and I turned to see him grinning down at me. I forced a smile and nodded.

When I turned back to Jet, I noticed that he'd stood up and taken a few steps toward to us. His eyebrows were furrowed as he studied me.

I forced a smile as I glanced around. It seemed as if everyone was interested in this strange girl that Crew and Jet seemed to know.

"Hi," Kate said, waving to everyone. "I'm Kate, and this is Brielle."

Crew's hand cupped my shoulder and he pulled me closer until I was sandwiched against him. "Out to see how the other side of town slums?"

I glanced up at him and nodded, not really sure how I was supposed to react.

"Let her go, Crew." Jet's voice sounded close. And when I peeked over, I realized that he *was* close. Like inches away.

Crew chuckled, and I could feel it reverberate in his chest. He squeezed me tight one more time before letting me go.

"Just trying to help the newbie feel welcome," he said as he dropped his arm and sauntered over to the table. He collapsed on a chair and took a long drink.

"You okay?" Jet asked. His voice was low, and I could hear the concern in it.

I nodded as I rubbed the part of my arm that Crew had touched. Even though I was happy to see Jet, I didn't belong here. At all.

"Come on, I'll get you a drink." Jet's fingertips brushed my arm, and I snapped my gaze over to him. What was he doing? Was he trying to touch me?

He must have noticed my reaction because he curled his fingers into his hand and dropped it next to his side. "Sorry," he said as he shoved his hands into his pockets.

"It's okay," I said. It was a lot more than okay. My whole body responded to his touch, and I wanted more. It was getting harder and harder to resist the urge to give myself over to him. To show the feelings that existed inside of me.

"Come on," he said, nodding toward the bar.

I glanced around for Kate only to find her in the corner, laughing at someone she knew. He was a tall kid with dark, curly hair. She looked preoccupied, so I nodded and followed after Jet.

Just as we passed by the group, I noticed the girl with dreadlocks staring at us. Her lips were pulled tight and her arms were crossed in front of her chest. She leaned over to another girl with black, curly hair and whispered something. Suddenly, curly-haired girl was staring at me as well.

I felt as if I was going to melt under their stare, so I picked up the pace and fell into step with Jet. He glanced down, and the soft smile he gave me warmed my cheeks.

"I'm happy you came," he said as he leaned against the bar and ordered two Sprites.

I slipped onto the barstool next to him and nodded. "Yeah. Kate seemed to think it was wise."

Jet grabbed a few pretzels from the bowl in front of us and slipped one into his mouth. He chewed it thoughtfully as he stared at me. "Why did she think it was wise?" he asked right before the bartender handed us our drinks.

Jet thanked him and paid. I moved to slip off the stool, but Jet pressed his hand on my knee. I froze as I felt the warmth of his fingertips against my bare skin. My heart took off, galloping in my chest.

"Wait," he said. His voice was deep and sent shivers across my skin. His hand lingered on my knee for a moment longer before he pulled it away.

My body felt cold in his absence.

"I just need a minute," he said as he leaned both elbows on the bar in front of him.

Worried about how I would sound if I spoke, I just nodded and entwined my fingers on my lap.

There was this palpable tension between us, and I wasn't sure how to interpret it. I decided that it would be best to just wait for Jet to tell me what this all meant.

He ate a few more pretzels before he leaned on one arm and turned his chest toward me. It was like he wanted to look at me. And from the expression on his face, he was taking me in.

My breath hitched in my throat as I peeked over at him.

He parted his lips a few times before pressing them shut. Was he struggling just as much as I was?

I shook my head slightly. With the number of girls staring at Jet tonight, I doubted that he had any trouble finding someone to care about him.

Who was I to this bad boy?

Jet was incredible. I couldn't be the only girl who saw that.

When I glanced back at Jet, I saw him staring at me in an open way that sent shivers across my skin. I felt exposed, and for the first time, I didn't hide from it. Maybe it was because I wanted to tell him exactly how I felt, even if I couldn't bring myself to utter the words.

I'd fallen hard for Jet. And even though we would be finished come Monday morning, I wanted him to know what he meant to me. What he would always mean to me.

He leaned in closer. I could smell his cologne and feel

the warmth emanating off of his chest. My senses were completely wrapped up in him. The whole world felt as if it were blurring around me. I was in one of those romantic movies where the only thing in focus is the couple.

Jet was all I wanted.

"You're a mystery," he said as his warm gaze met mine. I was so used to his dark and stormy intensity that, when he opened up, it took my breath away.

"I am?" I whispered. And then I cleared my throat. The band was starting up, so we were having to speak louder. "I am?" I yelled.

He nodded and then took a sip of his drink. "I can't figure you out." He met my gaze again. "And I want to."

Goosebumps rose up on my skin from the intensity of his words. Did they mean what I so desperately wanted them to?

"You do?" I asked.

The smile that played on his lips sent butterflies fluttering in my stomach. I felt so complete when I was around him. Like this was where I was meant to be.

Right here. Next to Jet.

He lifted his hand and brushed my hair from my shoulder. His fingers played against my neck, sending pulses of pleasure shooting through my entire body. He leaned in so close that I could feel his breath on my skin.

I closed my eyes as I took in what it felt like to be this close to Jet. To let my guard down and allow him in.

"You look beautiful," he whispered. There was this deep,

soulful sound to his voice that caused my breath to hitch in my throat.

My brain was officially a pile of mush.

"I am?" I asked.

Meet Brielle. The great conversationalist. But what could I do? Just being around Jet sent my entire body into shock. I couldn't process anything.

Jet pulled away and met my gaze again. He cupped his hand just below my ear. His thumb ran along my cheek in a soft manner. As if he were trying to memorize the curves of my face.

He nodded as he held my gaze. In that one look, I could see everything that he was trying to say. I could feel his feelings for me. He didn't need to say them. I knew he felt how I felt.

And it broke my heart.

CHAPTER FOURTEEN

*I*t feels so strange to go from pure euphoria to the pain of realizing that you can't have the one thing you want. It was like that feeling of descending in an airplane. You know you need to do it, but you hate the feeling of your stomach getting left in the sky.

That's how I felt as I studied the intensity with which Jet stared at me.

He liked me. And maybe a bit more than that.

But there was something nagging me in the back of my mind, telling me he couldn't.

We couldn't be together. He just didn't know that.

For some reason, I feared what he would say if he found out. If he realized that liking me was a fool's errand. I worried that he would choose to help his family rather than tell me to stay with him.

I'm not sure I could ever get over that. It was one thing

for me to give myself away for Jet's benefit. It was another thing to have him ask me to go.

I was pretty sure I wouldn't survive that conversation.

So I did the only thing I could think of—I pulled away. I broke the contact between us. I stood, almost stumbling off the bar stool as I put some distance between us.

Jet was left standing there with his hand raised like he wasn't sure what had just happened.

I gave him a weak smile, tucked my hair behind my ear, and told him I had to go to the bathroom. I needed to get away from him and the pain that was crushing my chest right now. Jet and I couldn't be anything, and I needed to accept that.

I'm not sure how I made it to the bathroom without breaking down, but I did. Maybe it was because I was in a bar, but people didn't seem too alarmed to see a half-crazed girl staggering to the bathroom.

I leaned against the sink as I put my head down and took some deep breaths. I fought the tears. I didn't want the last time Jet and I spent together to go this way. I wanted him to remember me in a good light. Not as a crazy, emotional wreck.

After a few calming breaths and some escaped tears, I gathered my emotions enough to look up and study my reflection. My face was splotchy and my eyes were puffy. I cupped my hands under the water and allowed them to fill up. Then I let the water splash back into the sink.

I took my wet fingers and dabbed under my eyes. I had a few minutes to compose myself before I needed to get back out there. I wanted to make sure I looked somewhat presentable.

The sound of the door opening caused my ears to twitch, but I was too distracted to look over my shoulder. It wasn't until someone laughed quietly behind me that I turned to find the dreadlocks girl staring at me.

"Jet," she said through her blue-covered lips.

I straightened and glanced over at her. Was she talking to me?

I just smiled and reached over to grab a paper towel. I dabbed at my eyes to remove the excess water there. I kept my gaze trained on myself in the mirror and silently prayed that she'd go away.

I didn't want talk to anyone about Jet right now, much less this stranger.

"He breaks your heart, doesn't he."

Well, I guess she didn't pick up on the fact that I didn't want to talk to her. She was watching me with her arms folded and an overly-lined eyebrow raised.

I forced a smile. "Do you know him?"

She scoffed and then turned to mess with her hair as she stared at her reflection. "He's my ex. Loser broke it off at the end of the school year."

I nodded, not sure what to say to that. "I'm sorry."

She shrugged. "His loss." Then she turned and stuck out her hand. "Name's Jasmine."

I gingerly shook her hand. "Brielle."

"Nice to meet you, Brielle." She turned back to the mirror. "Do I know you? I haven't seen you around."

I shook my head. "I'm staying at the Livingstone Hotel. I'm..." I wasn't sure how much I wanted to tell this stranger.

But it seemed like she was expecting me to finish my sentence. She turned and stared at me. "You're...?"

I fiddled with the hem of my dress and shrugged. "I'm here for the summer. I go to school in New York."

She parted her lips into an "o" shape. Then she nodded. "So, you're rich."

I almost choked on my spit. Call me crazy, but I really didn't want this girl to know anything about me. "I'm not. My parents are."

She let out a snort. "That's what rich people say."

I eyed the bathroom door, wondering if I could get out of here without her stopping me. Probably not. I ran track in school, but I wasn't that fast.

I was stuck in the bathroom with Jet's ex.

"Hey, so a group of us were going to sing this evening, but Deseree called in sick." She turned and rested her hip against the sink. "You any good?"

I coughed as I stared at her. "You mean sing?"

She nodded. "Just backup. Nothing too intense."

Truth was, I loved singing. I was in choir back home. And I was good. But I wasn't sure if I was singing-in-a-bar good. "Um..."

Her gaze turned expectant as she stared at me. I felt as if I couldn't say no.

So I nodded. "Sure." Besides, I wasn't at risk of getting too close to Jet if I was up on stage. It was probably for the best.

And it would put off the "I'm leaving for the summer and probably for good" conversation that I was going to have to have with him.

She cheered as she clapped her hands together. "Perfect! Come on," she said as she walked over to me and wrapped her arm around my shoulder.

I nodded, still feeling a tad awkward as she led me out of the bathroom.

We made our way through the crowded bar and over to the stage. I tried to ignore Jet's stare as we passed by him. His expression was a mixture of confusion and shock. I kept my gaze down, not sure how I was going to explain any of this to him.

When we got to the group of girls I'd seen Jasmine standing with earlier, she introduced me to them all. There were a few who seemed confused as to why I was there, but Jasmine reminded them of Deseree, and they all nodded in agreement.

I just smiled and kept to myself. I was ready to just sing the song and put this whole evening behind me. I didn't belong, and it was killing me to be this close to Jet and not tell him how I felt.

Maybe going to Italy was a good thing. Distance from Jet seemed to be the only thing that kept me somewhat sane.

"Let's go," Jasmine sang out as she pushed me toward the stage.

I stumbled as I tried to right myself in the ridiculous heels that Kate had me wear. By the time I got on to the stage, I was sure my face was beet red. Maybe from embarrassment. Maybe from nerves. I was getting up in front of all these strangers to sing something I hadn't prepared.

The reason for going on stage had left my mind, and the only thing I could think of was how badly I wanted to run away. How badly I wanted to go back in time and just stay at the hotel. That way, I wouldn't have met Jet and my heart wouldn't be breaking.

The opening notes to the song started up, and I glanced over to Jasmine, who gave me a big smile and a wink. I held onto the microphone on the stand in front of me like it was a lifeline. It took a few measures before I recognized the song.

My friend Portia from school was obsessed with nineties hits, which is the only reason why I recognized the song *That Boy is Mine* from Brandy and Monica.

I stared at Jasmine, wondering what the heck was going on. I barely knew the words to the song, but she didn't seem to be struggling. Instead, she was staring at me as she pulled the mic from its stand and began circling me. The other girls followed her, and I finally realized what she was up to.

She hadn't asked me up here to stand in for her friend. I was the target for her weird mean-girl prank.

And for some reason, all I could do was stand there. It was like my legs forgot how to move.

I could hear the laughter from the audience. My skin felt as if it were on fire. How could I have been so stupid? I never should have come. I should have stayed in the hotel with my parents, who didn't even know I was there. At least they didn't mock me.

Man...my life was pathetic. I couldn't get my parents to care about me, and I couldn't be with the one guy who decided that maybe he liked me, because I was leaving for freaking Italy on Monday.

How had things spiraled out of control so fast?

Suddenly, I felt an arm around my shoulder and a deep voice boomed in my ear, "Let's go."

I didn't even have to look to know who had come to my rescue.

Jet.

His hand felt warm as it pressed into my shoulder. He pulled me next to him like he was protecting me.

As soon as I felt him next to me, my body knew what to do. I walked with him across the stage and over to the stairs.

Jasmine protested, but Jet pushed right through her. I didn't look back as we made our way through the crowd and out to the parking lot. As the doors shut behind us, we slowed our pace.

"Wait," I said as I pulled out of his grasp and collapsed against the wall.

Jet stared at me as I grabbed my phone from my bra. "Kate," I said as I pulled up her number.

I waited for her to answer, praying she would hear her phone over the noise of the bar. From the angry look on Jet's face, there was no way he was just going to leave me alone. He was mad about what had happened in there, and I was pretty sure that I would spill everything if he asked.

And I didn't need that right now.

I didn't need his sympathy. I didn't need him to tell me not to go. And I certainly didn't need him to tell me *to* go.

The phone rang for what felt like an eternity. Finally, she answered.

"Bri? What *was* that? That tramp. I'm going to—"

"Hey, I'm outside. Can you come get me?"

There was a pause. "Are you with Jet?"

I closed my eyes and shook my head. "No," I said in the most unconvincing voice ever.

She snorted. "Have you talked to him?"

"Yes." Wow. Since when did I lie this much?

"I can tell you're lying. Talk to him. Tell him what you told me."

Tears pricked my eyes as I shook my head. I leaned into the phone so Jet couldn't hear me. "I can't."

"Brielle. Yes, you can. You have to. If the expression on his face when he realized what that stupid girl was doing was any indicator of how he felt about you, you need to tell him. He deserves to know."

I hated how right Kate was being right now. I knew I needed to tell Jet, I just wasn't ready for this all to be over. It felt so final.

"Okay," I whispered.

We said our goodbyes, and I hung up shoved the phone back into my dress. Jet was standing with his back to me, his hands shoved into his jacket pockets. He was staring up at the sky. I could tell he was upset from the way his shoulders were raised.

"What did she say?" he asked, not looking over at me.

I blinked back my tears as I stepped up to join him. We stood there, side by side, surrounded by silence. I didn't want to speak. The feeling of him standing next to me was exactly what I needed, and if I parted my lips, that would all be over.

When he glanced down at me, I realized he was waiting for me to speak. I sighed.

"She wants me to tell you the truth."

I could feel his gaze on me for a moment before he turned his attention back to the sky. "And what's that?"

The lump in my throat grew to the point that I feared I wouldn't be able to speak if I tried. I wanted to tell him, I did. But it was like my body was rejecting my decision.

"I can't do this," I said as I turned and walked away from him. "You need to stay away from me." I needed to get out of here. If I called Mrs. Porter she would probably be there in five minutes flat. I could leave. It would be so easy.

But just as I began to relax, two arms wrapped around me and suddenly I was airborne. I yelped as I whipped my head around to see Jet holding me with a very determined look on his face.

He pulled me to his chest and made his way across the parking lot to his bike.

"What are you doing?" I asked as I shifted to make sure that people couldn't see up my dress.

"Taking you with me," he growled as he set me down on his bike. Suddenly my choice of dress was coming back to bite me.

"My dress?" I said, motioning toward the hemline.

I swear Jet blushed as he stared at my legs. Then he shook off his jacket and set it on my lap.

"Here," he said. Then he grabbed his helmet and plopped it onto my head.

Before I could protest, he climbed onto the bike and started it up. The roaring sound of the engine filled my ears, silencing all my concerns. When I felt him shift to push the kickstand up, I wrapped my arms around his chest, allowing my body to remember what it felt like to be this close to him.

It was like holding him chased all my worries away.

He was exactly what I needed to calm down. To feel at peace.

I didn't fight him as he took off down the road. We rode together alongside the beach for what felt like forever. Or maybe I just wished it was. I wanted him to keep going and never stop. I wanted it to be just me and him. No family. No expectations. Just the two of us.

I wasn't sure how long he drove, but when he pulled into a small parking lot just off the ocean, I tried not to grumble. He killed the engine and pushed the kickstand down. He was off the bike before I could say anything.

I scrambled to get off as well. It was a feat to try to keep his jacket covering my legs. Once I was standing, Jet grabbed his coat and draped it over my shoulders. He took my hand, engulfing it in his.

He knew I was going to pull away if I was given the chance.

"Come with me," he said as he pulled me alongside him.

Since I had no idea where we were going, I followed.

We walked through the sand. The sound of the ocean crashing against the shore filled the night. At first, he walked faster than I did. Like he had a mission to accomplish.

Then he slowed, allowing our hands to fall to our sides. Maybe he realized that I wasn't going to go anywhere. How could I? My heart was pounding so hard, and yet, I felt complete walking next to him.

A few minutes later, a rundown shed appeared off to the side. It was hidden by some brush. I glanced over to Jet, but he didn't acknowledge me. Instead, he pulled on my arm as he made his way closer to it.

"What..." I started to ask, but Jet didn't stop. He opened the door and ushered me inside.

It looked better on the inside then it did on the outside. There was a small cot off in the corner. A few cans of food were lined up along a shelf. Candles dotted the other flat surfaces.

Jet motioned for me to sit on the cot as he pulled out a box of matches from underneath the bed. He struck one against the box and then made his way around the room, lighting the candles.

Soon, pale, flickering light filled the shed.

Jet threw the matches back under the bed.

Then he stood there like he didn't know what to do. He shoved his hands through his hair as he flicked his gaze from me to the wall behind my head.

I studied him, not sure what I should say. It had been a

whirlwind getting here, and I still wasn't certain why he'd brought me.

"I'm sorry," he said as he shoved his hands into his front pockets and finally met my gaze. His expression was sorrowful and caused my heart to break.

"For what?" My voice broke as emotions filled my chest. He had nothing to be sorry for.

"For what Jasmine did. I shouldn't have brought you to that place. It's..." He closed his eyes and shook his head. "I told you that you didn't fit in my life."

That stung. I blinked a few times, wondering if that was why he'd brought me here. But he could have told me this at the bar. He didn't need to drag me down to the beach to tell me that we would never work out.

"I'm sorry," I said and then winced. I could hear the hurt in my voice.

Jet glanced down at me and regret filled his gaze. "No. That's not what I meant." He blew out his breath as he scrubbed his face. "I just meant we don't work, you and I." He motioned between us.

Wow. That was worse.

Tears threatened to spill, so I stood. I just needed to get out of here before he pulled my heart from my chest and stomped on it. "I get it. It's okay. You don't have to worry about me," I said as I made my way over to the door.

"Brielle, I..." His hand grabbed mine, halting me in place.

I kept my gaze down, not sure if I could handle looking up at him.

"I'm an idiot."

Okay. This was different. I hesitated as I waited.

"You are so...perfect. And my life is a mess. I just..." His voice dropped off, and curiosity grew inside of me. I peeked over at him to see that he was staring at the ground.

"You just?" I turned to face him, pushing back my fear of opening up to him.

He stared at me for a moment before he closed the gap between us. He cradled my cheek in his hand, and, before I could breathe, he pressed his lips to mine.

CHAPTER FIFTEEN

The emotions that coursed through me as Jet pressed his lips to mine felt like heaven. Every part of my being responded to him. My lips moved in time with his. My hands felt the curves of his chest as they moved up to his shoulders and tangled in his hair.

His body pressed against mine, and every point of contact heated from his touch. I'd never felt more complete than I did when he wrapped his arms around my waist and pulled me closer.

I fell into kissing him. And I never wanted to stop falling.

"Brielle," he said as he pulled his lips away and pressed his forehead against mine.

"Mm-hmm," I mumbled as I dropped my hands back down to his chest. I could feel his pounding heart. It beat in time with my own.

"I—"

Panic filled me, and, before I knew what I was I doing, I pressed my finger to his lips. I couldn't hear those three little words. Once spoken, we couldn't take them back. "Please. Don't."

The look on his face caused my heart to crumble. I wanted to tell him what I'd been keeping from him before he confessed something like that.

"You don't know everything," I said.

Reality came crashing down on me as I pushed away from him. He tried to pull me back, but when I resisted, he let me go.

"What are you talking about?" he asked. His voice was full concern.

Keeping my gaze down, I made my way over to the cot and sat down. Maybe if I wasn't standing, we couldn't just pick up where we'd left off. My resolve to keep away from him was growing weaker by the second. "There's something I have to tell you."

It took a moment before he sat down next to me. I could feel his gaze as he stared at me, waiting for me to speak.

"Okay," he said.

I took a deep breath. Here went nothing. "I'm leaving for Italy," I said slowly.

I waited for him to respond. When he didn't, I continued.

"My parents want me to date this guy. He's the son of a business partner."

More silence.

Just as I parted my lips, Jet finally spoke.

"So are they bartering you?" There was a confused tone to his voice.

I felt the same. "Sort of."

Jet scoffed. "That's ridiculous. They can't expect you to go."

I nodded as tears filled my eyes. "I'm going," I whispered.

When he didn't respond, I glanced over at him.

"You're going? Why?" His forehead was furrowed as he studied me.

A tear slipped down my cheek, and I reached up and angrily wiped it off. "You won't understand." I hated saying that, but I didn't want him to have to choose between his family or me.

I was already having to do that, and it was pulling me apart inside.

He reeled back at my words. It broke my heart that he looked so betrayed. "Why wouldn't I understand?"

I swallowed. My emotions choked my throat as my mind raced. How could I explain this to him?

"There's a lot riding on this deal. If I don't go, things could change. Lives would be altered." I peeked over at him. His face had only hardened more.

"Do you love the guy?" He stared down at me as if challenging me to answer.

I met his gaze and held it for a moment before I slowly shook my head. "No."

He shrugged as he leaned closer. "Then that's it. There's no question. This is the twenty-first century. That kind of

180 | ANNE-MARIE MEYER

stuff is in the past. I'm sure there are other ways for your family to form partnerships."

If only. But Jet didn't know my parents. They were going to make sure that the Livingstone empire stayed in the family, by any means necessary.

He must have read my response on my face because he scoffed and stood. "So that's it? You're not going to fight this? I mean, come on." He swallowed so hard that I could see his Adam's apple bob up and down. It was tearing him up inside, and I hated that.

I reached up and grabbed his hand, reveling in the freedom touching him brought. I mean, I'd spent the whole day fighting my feelings for him, but now I could reach out and entwine my fingers with his. Like it was as natural as breathing.

"I'm not leaving until Monday. We can still spend tomorrow together. It'll be fine." Even as the words escaped my lips, I knew things were not going to be fine. I was pretty sure my heart was going to break into a million pieces.

"But..." His voice drifted off as he closed his eyes for a moment and then glanced down at me. "Brielle," he said as he sat back down on the cot. He folded my hand in both of his and glanced over at me. "I don't want to let you go."

I rested my free hand on his and nodded. "I know. It's okay. You'll be just fine. I promise."

And I did promise. If I went to Italy, then the deal would go through. Brit and his mom would get better jobs. They could get out of the slums they were living in. It would be perfect.

He slipped his hand out from under mine and reached up to tuck my hair behind my ear. "But who will drive me crazy?" he asked as he brought his hand back to cup my cheek. He ran his thumb over my lips, and all I could do was respond by leaning into his hand.

I felt so safe here. Like no matter what, Jet was going to take care of me, protect me. For the first time in my life, I felt wanted. I felt like I belonged, and that was all I'd ever wished for.

"I'm sure you'll find someone else," I whispered. The words physically hurt to say, but they were true. Jet was amazing. Any girl would be lucky to have him.

His finger pressed against my lips. "I won't ever find someone quite like you," he said as he slid his finger down and pressed his lips to mine.

My tears flowed freely now, and Jet must have noticed because he pulled back with a concerned expression. He reached up and gingerly wiped each cheek.

"When you cry, it makes me want to kill whoever is hurting you," he said, his voice gruff and full of meaning.

I shook my head. "Don't," I said as I reached up to hold one of his hands. I brought it down to rest in my lap.

"Brielle, I can't help it. I need to protect you. I think it was what I was born to do." He leaned in and rested his forehead against mine. "I was meant to find you outside the hotel."

I laughed as I glanced up at him. "Why were you there anyway?"

He pulled back and a strained look flashed in his eyes. "My dad. I figured he might head back to the hotel once he got more liquor inside of him. I was waiting to see if he came back." He glanced over at me. "I'm glad I did."

I pulled his hand up and wrapped it around my shoulders. He must have known what I was trying to do because he shifted and pushed until he was leaning against the wall. I followed him, bringing my feet up and resting my head on his chest.

His arm was warm and tight against my body as he held me. I could feel the beating of his heart, but this time, it was slow and steady. I tapped my fingers on his chest in time with it.

"What are you doing?" he asked. His chuckle rumbled in his chest.

"I like your heartbeat," I said.

He reached up and engulfed my hand in his, stilling my movement. "I'm glad I can please you."

Heat flushed my face as my eyes widened. He laughed. "Dirty mind, little one."

I shrugged. "Sorry."

His laughter died down and silence filled the little shack. It wasn't awkward or filled with words not spoken. It was just calm. For the first time all day, I could breathe.

Sure, my future was still set in stone. Plans were still in motion. But right now, lying with Jet, listening to his heartbeat, and feeling him breathing, I was happy.

This was where I belonged.

"Thank you," I whispered.

I felt Jet shift as he looked down at me. "For what?"

"For letting me get on your bike. For taking care of me. For showing me your life."

"You sound like you're dying."

For all intents and purposes, I was. My future was all planned out, and it didn't include him.

"Before I forget..." I shifted until I was half-sitting, resting my weight on my hand. I reached into my bra, and Jet's eyebrows shot up.

I gave him an exasperated look, and he just shrugged.

"The money I owe you," I said as I pulled out the twenties and pressed them into his free hand.

He started at me for a moment and then back down to his hand. "What?"

I snuggled back into his chest. "You need it more than I do. Besides, we had a deal."

I wasn't sure, but it felt like Jet suddenly stiffened. I glanced up to see his jaw was set and his gaze had turned stony.

"What?" I asked.

He glanced down at me. "I don't want this," he said, handing the money back over.

I stared at him. "What?"

He met my stare head on. "I don't want your money."

"But, Jet—"

He shook his head as he slipped off the cot. "Brielle, are you serious?"

I sat there, the coolness of the air hitting me, but I didn't really notice. The punch to the gut was stronger. "I promised you," I said.

His jaw clenched as he glanced around the shed as if he were trying to figure out what to say. "It's not about the money. It's not about a promise. I..." He knitted his eyebrows together like he was hoping I'd pick up on what he was trying to say.

But I wasn't going to listen. It didn't matter how he felt. He needed the money. For him. For Cassidy. For Brit. I wasn't going to let his pride dictate whether or not he took this money. I made a promise and I was going to keep it.

"You're being ridiculous," I said as I gathered the bills and slipped them back into my bra.

He scoffed. "I doubt that."

I stared at him. "You need this. For Cassidy? For Brit?" I tucked my hair behind my ears as I met his gaze. "You can't afford to act like this."

He met my gaze as if he were trying to challenge me back. "I can take care of my family."

I knew that was true. I sighed as I nodded. "I know. I guess, I just wanted to help out too."

His expression softened and his shoulders slumped. He sat back down on the cot and glanced over at me. "I know," he said.

He leaned back on the headboard and brought his arm up. He tapped his chest, and I hesitated before I snuggled up next to him.

I sighed as I drew circles around on his sternum. "That was crazy."

"Hmm?"

I laughed, the memory of the day washing over me. "I never thought that I would meet a guy and fall in love with him on the same day." My fingers stopped moving as soon as the words left my lips. I hadn't meant for them to come out, but there they were, hanging in the air.

Jet's grip tightened, and I felt him move so he could stare down at me.

"Fall in love?"

I closed my eyes for a moment. I wanted to take the words back and loved the fact that he'd heard them all at the same time.

He pulled me closer to his chest. "Do you love me, Brielle?"

I pinched my lips shut, fearing what else I was going to confess. "No," I whispered.

"Lie. I heard you." He pushed me up so he could see my face.

I kept my gaze down, fearing what looking at him would do to me. But he wasn't going to let this go. Instead, he pressed his finger under my chin and tipped my face up until I had to look at him.

"Do you love me?" he asked again.

Heat rushed to my cheeks, giving away my feelings. He held my gaze, and I could see the earnestness there. He wanted—no, needed—to know.

"Yes," I whispered.

He straightened as his expression turned intense. He leaned close to me, until he was only inches from my face. "I love you too," he whispered.

A shudder rushed through my body as his words engulfed me. It was exactly what I wanted to hear and what I feared. I needed his love like I needed air to breathe. He was my lifeline in my crazy, depressing world.

I met his gaze, and, before either of us could speak, I leaned forward and pressed my lips to his. This time, I kissed him with all the feeling inside of me. Our lips moved in unison as we explored and devoured the other.

We kissed like it was the last time we would ever kiss. Because come Monday morning, that was going to be true.

But right now, we were two lost souls who'd found their missing half, and we were going to make every second we had left count.

I'm not sure when we fell asleep. We spent most of our time together snuggling on the cot and telling each other stories. There were a few times that I could remember Jet shaking me awake, telling me I'd fallen asleep.

I must have done it again, but he didn't wake me up.

It wasn't until the sun streamed in from the small window in the back that I finally woke up. My neck felt crimped and achy.

I winced as I pulled myself up, rubbing my strained muscles.

Jet's head was tipped to the side and his eyes were closed. It was like his arm was stuck in its position, and I could see where my ear had made a mark on his skin.

I softly giggled as I stared at him. Even in the morning, with the sun streaming down on him, he was the best-looking guy I'd ever seen.

And he cared about me.

My heart sang.

He must have heard me because he shifted on the bed and peeked through one eye. "Morning?" he asked.

I nodded. "Looks that way."

He groaned in protest as he shifted until he was no longer propped up but was lying down on the bed. "It's way too early."

I nodded as I reached out and rested my hand on his chest. He mumbled under his breath but brought his hand up to wrap around my fingers. He held my hand as his eyes drifted closed.

I wished we could stay there forever, just me and him in this shed. But we couldn't. I was leaving in less than twenty-four hours, and we were going to make the most of it.

"Come on," I said as I tapped his shoulder.

He groaned again but sat up, keeping his eyes closed. "You're mean in the morning."

I shrugged as he stood. "We've got less than a day to spend together. We are going to do everything."

His shoulders slumped as he turned to face me, his eyes now slits. "You're still going?" he asked.

I put on a brave face and nodded. "Of course. It's my duty," I said, trying to make light of the situation by striking a superhero pose.

He didn't look amused as he stared back at me. "Haha, you're not that funny."

I swatted his arm as I climbed off the bed. "I am too," I said.

He shook his head.

I waved away his response as I tiptoed over to my shoes and slipped them on. Then I folded my arms as I watched him hunt for his jacket. "Thanks for bringing me to your secret hideout."

He turned to look at me, an unamused expression on his face. "You make me sound like a twelve-year-old boy with a sign that says *no girls allowed.*"

I laughed, imagining twelve-year-old Jet with a dirt stained face and a spear he'd whittled himself. "Ah, that explains it," I said, everything suddenly coming into place.

He furrowed his brow. "What?"

I shrugged. "You. The stick." I mimicked him scraping the piece of wood outside the hotel yesterday.

Jet grabbed his jacket and slipped it on. "Do you always talk crazy this early in the morning?"

I shrugged. "I'm not normally around other people this early in the morning, so I have no clue." Then I waved to his jacket. "What are you doing?" I asked, motioning toward my dress. Why I was stupid enough to wear this thing last night confounded me.

"Ah," he said as he bent down and pulled out a plastic tub. He reached inside and grabbed what looked like a pair of sweatpants. "Here," he said, throwing them my direction. "Maybe next time wear a dress you can ride a bike in."

I scoffed as I shook the pants out and then slipped them on over my dress. "I wasn't expecting to come to your love hut last night."

He chuckled. "Love hut?"

"Yeah. I'm assuming you bring all of your girlfriends here."

He stopped moving to turn and stare at me. "All my girlfriends?"

This was a fun conversation. "Do you do this a lot? Repeat what the other person said?"

He snorted. "Only when they are talking crazy. Do you hear what you're saying?"

Why was it so unrealistic for me to think he had a lot of girlfriends? "You're saying you don't date a lot?"

He pushed his hands through his hair. "I'm kind of honored that you think I'm this guy that gets all the girls, but no, I'm not some ladies' man and this isn't my love hut."

I studied him. He was serious. "Then why the secret shed on the beach?"

He glanced around and then his uneasy gaze settled on me. "This is where I run to when things get out of hand with Dad." He shrugged as he stuffed his hands into his jacket pockets. "This is my safe haven."

I studied his furrowed brow and downturned lips. Then my feelings for him heightened as his words washed over me. He was sharing this with me.

He was letting me in. Trusting me.

And yet, here I was, keeping something important from him.

Man, I was a jerk.

"My parents are partnering with the family they want me to go to Italy with so they can build those hotels they were talking about on the news." The words tumbled from my lips.

Jet stopped moving to study me. "What?"

"That's why…"

He kept his gaze on me for a moment before he crossed the floor, stopping inches from me. "Is that why you have to go?"

I glanced up at him. My lips parted as I took in his frustrated gaze. I didn't trust my voice, so I just nodded. "Yes."

He growled as he stared at me. "That's ridiculous, Brielle. You can't just live your life for other people. For me." He wrapped his arm around my waist and pulled me close. "Do what *you* want to do."

I reached up and rested my hand on his chest. I could feel his warmth on my fingertips. I wanted this. All of this.

But I also wanted to help his family, and I knew in the long run that would make him happiest.

"It's what I want," I whispered.

He held me close for a moment before he let me go. I tried not to read into the fact that he couldn't meet my gaze. Pain was etched across his expression.

Instead, I pushed my hair from my face and smiled at him.

"Let's go," he said, keeping his gaze on the ground.

I nodded and allowed him to open the door for me. I

stepped out into the morning sun, trying to make myself feel better about all of this. But I felt terrible.

My last day here in Atlantic City with Jet was going just great.

Not.

CHAPTER SIXTEEN

*W*e walked in silence to Jet's bike. I wasn't sure what to say to him. I could tell he was upset with me. That he wanted me to say that I didn't have to go to Italy. That I had a choice, even though I knew that wasn't the case.

I couldn't stay if it meant his family would be hurt. I cared too much about them. If only he saw that, then things would be different.

Why couldn't he just see that I was doing this for him?

Just as we neared his bike, my phone chimed. I pulled it out; Mrs. Porter had texted me.

Intrigued, I swiped my screen on and read her text.

Mrs. Porter: I think you should get back here.

I stared at her words. Why would she say that? I'd already agreed with Mom and Dad that I would come back tonight.

Me: What's up?

I waited for her to respond. Jet took the time to inspect his bike.

Mrs. Porter: Things are happening. You should get back.

I loved Mrs. Porter. She was like a second mother to me. So the fact that she was asking me to come home worried me. Normally, she'd support my decision to stay out. To live my life before my parents forced me to live the life they'd picked for me.

Me: Be there in five.

She texted me a thumbs up, and I slid my phone back into my bra. I turned to see Jet leaning against a nearby fence. He had his legs stretched out in front of him and his hands shoved into his pockets. He looked so thoughtful, staring out at the ocean.

I hated interrupting him when he looked this calm. But I needed to get home.

"Can we stop by the hotel?" I asked as I walked over to him. "I could use a clean pair of clothes and a good teeth brushing."

Jet glanced over at me. "Do you think that's a good idea?"

I furrowed my brow. My parents were controlling, but they weren't the type to lock their daughter in a dungeon. "I'm sure it'll be fine. Besides, they know I'm not coming back until tonight, and they're okay with that." I linked arms with him and then leaned my head on his shoulder. "I'll be fine."

He sighed and I felt his shoulder sag under me. Then he nodded. "Okay. Let's get this over with."

The ride back to the hotel was faster than I expected. I

194 | ANNE-MARIE MEYER

felt as if I blinked, and suddenly, he was pulling into the alley behind the hotel and turning off his engine. He glanced over his shoulder at me. I slipped off the helmet and climbed off his bike.

I took a deep breath as I handed the helmet over to him and straightened my hair. "I'll be back. I promise."

He held onto the helmet and nodded. "Of course." He gave me a soft smile and an encouraging look.

I soaked in as much of Jet Miller as I could before I turned and headed toward the back door of the hotel. The exact spot that I'd come out yesterday.

No one seemed to notice me as I walked through the kitchen and out to the lobby. I nodded to a few people that I'd been introduced to but didn't really know. Once I got to the elevator, I pressed the up button.

It wasn't too long before I was standing in front of the penthouse, staring at the door. I knew I should just go inside, I just felt as if I needed to prepare myself for whatever was happening on the other side.

I took a deep breath and turned the handle. Of course, it was locked, so I raised my hand to knock. I knew the code, but I felt as if I'd be intruding. A few seconds later, the door opened and Mrs. Porter stood on the other side.

Her eyes widened as she took me in. "What happened to you?" she asked as she stepped back and let me enter.

I scoffed as I slipped off my shoes. "Geez, I missed you, too," I said.

Mrs. Porter laughed as she reached out and pulled me into a hug. "I missed you."

We embraced, and then I pulled back, glancing around. "Where are they, and what's with the cryptic message?"

She tapped her lips with her finger as she nodded toward Mom and Dad's room. "She's back there. But you should get changed before you see her. She's under a lot of stress, and I don't think this"—she waved to Jet's sweatpants —"will help."

I shook my head. The last thing I cared about right now was pleasing my parents. I was here for a quick change and to brush my teeth and then I was headed back out. "I'm not here for that," I said as I slipped past her and made my way toward my bedroom door.

Mrs. Porter didn't seem pleased by my response. I could hear her footsteps as she followed after me. But I didn't want to hear her excuses for my parents.

I entered my room and shut the door. I sat down at my vanity and winced at my hair and makeup. I felt bad that Jet had to stare at me this morning. I was not the kind of person that looked amazing when they woke up.

After I pulled a hairbrush through my hair and wiped my makeup from my face, I felt more refreshed. I dressed in a pair of jean shorts and a breezy top.

If I was going to spend my last day with Jet, I was going to be comfortable.

This time I dumped all my necessities into my purse— despite Mom's voice nagging me in the back of my mind— and slipped on my sandals.

When I opened my door, Mrs. Porter was still standing there with an annoyed look on her face.

"I'm spending the day out," I said as I nodded to her and headed into the bathroom.

Mrs. Porter wouldn't give up. "I really think you should talk to your parents."

I stared at her as I prepped my toothbrush and then stuck it in my mouth.

"Jackie," Mom's voice filled the air and caused my stomach to flip upside down.

Mrs. Porter's eyes widened as she stepped away from the door and Mom appeared.

"Who are you talking to?" Mom asked as she studied Mrs. Porter and then turned to stare at me. "Oh. You're home."

Yep. That sounded about right.

"I'm not staying," I said as I quickly brushed my teeth and turned on the water to rinse out my mouth. Still feeling gross, I stuck the toothbrush back in for one more scrub down.

"Oh, stop being so dramatic." Mom folded her arms. "Your little runaway act could have cost us the deal with the Espositos."

"I don't want to talk about this." My voice was muffled by the toothpaste and brush.

Mom sighed in her *Brielle is acting up again* way. "Well, then I guess I shouldn't tell you that the Italy trip is off."

Just as the last words left her lips, I spit toothpaste everywhere. I pulled the toothbrush from my mouth as my jaw fell open.

"Brielle," Mom scolded me as she wiped toothpaste from her suit coat. "Come on. Be a lady."

"Go back," I said after spitting into the sink. "What did you say?"

Mom sighed. "Always the dramatics with you." She leaned in. "You don't have to go to Italy. The Espositos signed on. No stipulations."

She nodded at me and then pointed to her lips as she made her way out of the bathroom.

I rinsed the sink quickly, dried off my face, and stuck my toothbrush into the drawer. My heart was racing a mile a minute as I ran after her.

"Mom," I said, my voice rising with frustration.

Mom turned. "What?"

"What...? How...?" I couldn't figure out the right words in my mind.

Mom sighed as she pulled out a water bottle from the fridge and twisted off the cap. "Apparently, Stefano couldn't keep his pants on. He was caught with"—Mom cleared her throat as her face went red—"a married woman. To keep things quiet, the Espositos agreed to sign with us. End of story."

My brain was slowly processing what she'd said. So, instead of having a marriage to hang over the Espositos head, my parents now had dirt on their son. To my parents it was potato-potahto. Whatever they needed to do to get the job done, they would do it.

"So...I don't have to go to Italy?"

Mom set the water bottle down on the counter. "You don't have to go to Italy."

My ears were ringing. "Why didn't you tell me sooner?"

Mom let out an exasperated sigh. "You told us not to bother you. You said you'd be back by tonight. We figured we'd tell you when we saw you next."

I wanted to feel frustrated at my parents. I wanted to tell them that I couldn't believe they would keep something like this from me. But I didn't want to jinx it. If this was the truth, then I was going to take it, no questions asked.

I couldn't contain my excitement. I pumped my fists in the air and then danced around the kitchen. I grabbed Mom and pulled her into a hug—despite her protests.

"Brielle, please. I'll have to get this dry-cleaned," she said as she pulled away and smoothed out her skirt.

I didn't care. I was free. I wasn't going to Italy. I didn't have to marry creepy-Stefano. The deal was done. The hotels were getting built. And I...

Jet.

"I have to go. I'll be back later," I said as I grabbed my purse and headed toward the door.

"Wait, Brielle. Where are you going?"

I paused and turned around. Mom's earnest face caused me to stop. It'd been a long time since I'd heard Mom ask me anything when it wasn't followed up by, *this is what we want you to do for us.*

"I met someone," I said, drawing the words out.

Mom's eyebrows instantly went up. "Like a boy someone?"

I sighed and nodded.

Mom pinched her lips together and shook her head. "No. Not okay." She started to pace in front of the sink. Then she stopped and pointed her finger at me. "Who is this boy?"

Courage built up inside of me. Jet's voice was ringing in my ears. He was here to protect me—which meant I could protect me too. His faith in me was giving me the strength to finally stand up to Mom.

"He lives on the other side of town. You won't like him, I can guarantee it, but I don't care."

Mom steepled her fingers as she studied me. "We have standards and an image to uphold. It doesn't sound like he will uphold the Livingstone name."

I held up my hand, silencing her. I wasn't going to stand for this. Jet protected me; I was going to protect him. "I don't care about that. He's the one for me. He…gets me." I couldn't help the smile that twitched my lips.

Mom groaned. "Brielle, you two barely know each other. How can you trust that he isn't out to get something from you? Our family has money, which means you need to be more discerning with who you decide to associate with."

I thought of everything Jet had done for me. I thought of the wad of cash I'd tried to give him. Whatever Mom thought about Jet, I knew the truth.

He wasn't only someone I could trust, he was the man I loved. Nothing was going to get in the way of that. Definitely not Mom and Dad. They were going to have to make a decision about Jet for themselves. But for me, he was exactly what I wanted in my life.

"I gotta go," I said as I shot her a quick smile and walked over to the door.

Mom was still trying to process what had just happened.

I reached the door, turned the handle, and stopped. I thought of Jet and his parents who didn't seem to be that dedicated to him. Then I thought of Mom standing there with a shocked expression.

It felt good to stand up to her. To tell her what I was going to do instead of asking for permission. But I wanted a better relationship with my parents. If my time with Jet taught me anything, it was that family was important. They were all I had.

So I turned and walked back over to Mom and pulled her into a hug. She stiffened but didn't pull away. I pressed my lips to her cheek and then leaned back.

"Love you, Mom. I'll be back later."

Mom peeked over at me and then nodded. "I love you too, Brielle," she said. She reached out her hand and rested it on my elbow. Then she smiled.

Probably one of the only genuine smiles I'd seen from her in a long time.

She squeezed my arm. "When you get back, you bring that boy up here. Dad and I are going to want to talk to him."

My stomach twisted as her words settled around me. But she was offering an olive branch, and I was going to take it.

I nodded. "Of course."

She gave me a quick smile and then waved her hand toward the door. "He's probably waiting."

I ran through the door and over to the elevator as fast as I could. I pressed the down button and waited for it to open.

It felt like an eternity as I stood in the elevator, waiting for the doors to open and the lobby to come into view. When the doors parted, I bolted toward the back alley, where I hoped Jet was still waiting for me. For some reason, the thought that he'd decided I wasn't worth the drama crossed my mind.

As soon as I burst outside, I scanned the area where I'd left him.

Nothing.

I muscled down the fear that I might never see him again and began to search between the dumpsters.

"Jet?" I called out as I desperately tried to keep calm.

Nothing.

"Jet?" I called again.

I turned around to glance behind me. When I turned back around, I was suddenly enveloped in Jet's arms.

"Hey," he said, smiling down at me.

I squealed as I wrapped my arms around his neck and buried my face into his skin, breathing in his scent. Everything seemed that much sweeter. Everything felt that much better now that I was staying.

Jet was mine, and I could be his...if he still wanted me.

Worry settled in my stomach as I pulled away to study

202 | ANNE-MARIE MEYER

him. He set me down and quirked an eyebrow as his gaze roamed my face.

"Everything okay?" he asked.

I blinked a few times, trying to process my feelings. I was about to have everything I wanted. But for some reason, I couldn't help but think that he'd confessed those feelings to me because he knew I was leaving. Would he feel the same now that I was staying?

I chewed my lip as I thought of how to ask him.

"Brielle, what's wrong?" he asked, dipping down to catch my gaze.

"What if I told you I was staying."

He pulled back, his gaze intensifying. "What?"

I swallowed, hoping I wasn't about to mess up the one good thing that I had in my life. The one guy who'd finally cared about me.

"Mom just told me that I don't have to go. Apparently, Stefano was sleeping with a married lady in our hotel. My parents have proof. The Espositos agreed to sign with my parents to keep it out of the media." As the words tumbled from my lips, Jet just stood there with a confused look on his face.

He blinked a few times. "Wow. Um, that's a lot to take in."

I nodded and then glanced down at my hands. Was it weird that I wanted him to gather me into his arms and tell me how important I was to him? That he was grateful that I wasn't going? The longer he just stood there, staring at me, the more insecure I felt.

"Brielle," he said as he pressed his finger under my chin and tipped my face up until I had no choice but to look at him. "Why do you look worried?"

Emotions clung to my throat as I stared at him. I didn't want to seem clingy, but I also wanted to be honest. I loved him, and all I wanted was for him to feel the same, even without the threat of me leaving hanging over us.

"I'm worried it will change how you feel about me." I forced a smile. I wanted him to know I wasn't going to pressure him, no matter how he felt.

Falling in love over a 24-hour period of time felt like a fantasy. But I couldn't deny how I felt about him.

"Why would you staying change the way I felt about you?"

Shivers rushed across my skin as he wrapped his arm around my waist and pulled me closer. He dipped down and pressed his lips against the top of my head.

"I don't know. I mean, it was romantic and spontaneous to say you love me when I'm leaving. Will you be able to handle it if I stick around?"

Jet leaned back as he stared at me. "No. Will you be able to handle me?"'

I snorted as I reached out and rested my hands on his chest. I could feel the beating of his heart. I'd memorized the cadence. It was so familiar to me.

"I don't see that happening," I said as I glanced up at him. I hoped he could feel my meaning.

His brows furrowed as he tipped his forehead down and

rested it on mine. "I'll stay until you tell me to go," he murmured.

Butterflies raced around in my stomach as I slid my hands up to his shoulders and threaded my fingers together at the base of his neck. "Promise?" I asked, tipping my lips toward his.

He nodded as he leaned in and brushed his lips against mine. "Promise."

"Forever?"

He nodded and pressed his lips to mine again—this time with more passion than I'd ever felt. Pulses of pleasure rushed from my lips and exploded down to my toes. Never had my life felt so perfect.

I belonged to Jet, and he belonged to me.

Sure our future wasn't certain and we still had trials ahead—namely meeting my parents—but there was no one I'd rather do this with.

Jet was my person—now and forever.

He pulled back, his cocky half-smile returning. He reached up and cradled my cheek with his hand.

"Forever."

He stepped back, running his hands down the back of my arms and then entwining his fingers in mine. He smiled down at me as he nodded toward his bike.

"Come on," he said as he let go of one hand and guided me over. He grabbed the helmet and handed it to me.

"Where are we going?" I asked as I slipped the helmet on and buckled it under my chin.

He chuckled as he swung a leg over the seat.

I kept ahold of his shoulders as I climbed on the back.

"Does it matter?" he asked, tipping his head back so I could hear him.

No, it didn't matter. As long as I was with him, I was happy. And I was determined to be happy this summer.

"Not to me," I said as I slid my hands around his sides, pressing against him as I entwined my fingers.

He started the bike and it roared to life. I held on as he pulled out of the alleyway and onto the main road.

I closed my eyes as we sped down the road. It wasn't because I was scared or nauseous, it was because I was happy. Jet completed me in a way I never knew I could feel.

This was where I belonged.

EPILOGUE

I didn't know why I was nervous as I sat on my bed. My suitcase was packed and sitting next to me. I tapped my fingers on my leg as I glanced around.

I could hear the ticking of the clock on the wall as the moment I was to leave for New York drew closer and closer.

Jet and I had a whirlwind summer. We spent every spare moment we could together. Mom and Dad weren't too happy at first, but when Jet showed up for dinner in a button-up shirt and tie, Dad snorted—which was about as close to acceptance as he gets—and they were more receptive to the idea of Jet and I dating.

Dad even offered Jet a job in the hotel.

Which worked for me. I mean, he wanted to work, and I knew that regardless of how Dad felt about our relationship, he took care of his employees. It made me happy to know that while I was gone, Dad and Mom would look after him.

There was a soft knock on the door. I glanced over to see Jet standing in the doorway. His hair was slicked down, and he had on a light-blue uniform with the words Livingstone Hotel stitched on the breast pocket.

My heart jumped in my chest as I stood and ran over to him.

Jet's smile made my stomach flip-flop. He wrapped his arms around me and pulled me up. I giggled as I pressed my lips to his. I lost myself in that kiss. It amazed me that no matter how many times we kissed, it always felt different.

Real.

When we pulled apart, Jet slowly lowered me to the ground but kept his arms protectively wrapped around me.

"What am I going to do without you here?" he asked as he pressed his forehead against mine.

I giggled as I pressed my hands to his chest, sprawling out my fingers so I could feel his warmth and his beating heart. "I'm not sure," I whispered.

Truth was that I didn't know what I was going to do without Jet.

I was a nomad, moving from place to place, not really knowing where I belonged. But when I was wrapped in Jet's arms, feeling his familiar heartbeat and warmth surround me, I knew I was home. He was everything I needed to feel complete.

"That's not too comforting," he said. His voice had grown deeper, and it sent shivers down my body.

"You're coming to New York."

He pulled back, his eyebrow quirked. "I am?"

I nodded. Nerves rushed through me—I wasn't sure how he was going to react.

"Mom and Dad said they would come spend Christmas with me. I asked if they could bring you, and…" I raised my eyebrows as I met his gaze.

"I'm going to fly with your parents?" he asked.

I paused, trying to judge his reaction before I slowly nodded.

The silence that engulfed us was almost deafening. I knew my parents struggled with the fact that I was dating him, but I figured that these last few months had changed that.

He reached his hand up and cradled my cheek. "Promise you won't replace me with someone in New York?"

I stared at him. I couldn't believe he was asking me that. "What?"

He shrugged. "I'm worried you'll get to New York with all those fancy people and forget me."

I pressed my lips into his hand. "Not possible," I said as I glanced up at him.

He held my gaze before he slowly nodded. "Then I will be there. For you."

I giggled as I rose up onto my tiptoes and pressed my lips against his.

We kissed until there was a staccato knock on the door. I turned to see Mrs. Porter standing there with an iPad in the crook of her arm. She was slowly lowering her hand. "It's time," she said.

I pulled away from Jet, and before I could grab my suitcase, Jet beat me to it.

"Hey," I said. "I could have done that."

He winked at me. "I know."

I shook my head but didn't fight the smile that emerged. We walked out into the hallway. When we got to the kitchen, Mom was standing by the counter, studying her phone. She must have heard us because she glanced up as we approached.

The smile that emerged seemed genuine, and I couldn't help but feel happy. So much had changed this summer that I was beginning to wonder if it had all been real.

Mom and Dad were trying to be more involved. I had Jet. I really couldn't imagine my life going any better.

"How are you, Mr. Miller?" Mom asked, nodding in Jet's direction. She held out her hand and they shook.

"Good. Thanks, Mrs. Livingstone," Jet said.

To the untrained eye, their exchange seemed stiff. But not to me. I knew Mom was trying.

After they dropped hands, she turned to me. "Ready?" she asked.

I nodded. Mom had agreed to drop one of her meetings so she could accompany me to the airport—her words not mine.

"Yes," I said, slipping my gaze over to Jet, who was studying me. The intensity in his gaze as he studied me caused butterflies to take flight.

Mom nodded to Jet and me and then made her way out toward the elevator. Mrs. Porter followed.

I glanced up at Jet to see his forehead furrowed and a twinge of sadness in his gaze.

"Will you miss me?" he asked, reaching up to tuck my hair behind my ear.

I nodded. "Every day."

He dipped down to brush his lips against mine. "I love you, Brielle."

I couldn't help the tear that escaped and rolled down my cheek. Jet reached up and gently brushed it away.

I was going to miss him. It was going to feel like a piece of me was missing these next few months. "I love you, too, Jet."

He kissed me again. This time deeper and more passionate than I'd ever experienced. I lost myself in the feeling of my body pressed against his. In the joining of our two souls. We'd been wandering, not knowing where we were going.

But over that one day. That one, 24-hour period, we'd found each other.

And we were never going to let go.

***

I hoped you love Brielle and Jet's story. I love bad boys and the trope, enemies to lovers. It so fun to write their progression as they fall in love.

Up next in the rules of love series, is Scarlet and heart throb, Cayden Rivers.

Scarlet is the daughter of a movie producer and her mom insists that she spend the summer visiting her dad. What she didn't expect was to meet teen heart throb, Cayden Rivers.

And she certainly didn't expect to end up fake dating him.

Discover how they break the rules in
Rule #5: You Can't Fall for Your Fake Summer Fling
I thought I was strong enough to go along with the plan. Fake dating heart throb, Cayden Rivers, seemed simple enough.
Apparently not.
HERE!

JOIN THE NEWSLETTER

Want to learn about all of Anne-Marie Meyer's new releases plus amazing deals from other authors?
Sign up for her newsletter today and get deals and giveaways!
PLUS a free novella, Love Under Contract
TAKE ME TO MY FREE NOVELLA!

Also join her on these platforms:

Facebook

Instagram

anne-mariemeyer.com

Printed in Great Britain
by Amazon